The Great Dimpole Oak

A Richard Jackson Book

The GREAT DIMPOLE OAK

by JANET TAYLOR LISLE

Drawings by

STEPHEN GAMMELL

ORCHARD BOOKS NEW YORK LONDON

A division of Franklin Watts, Inc.

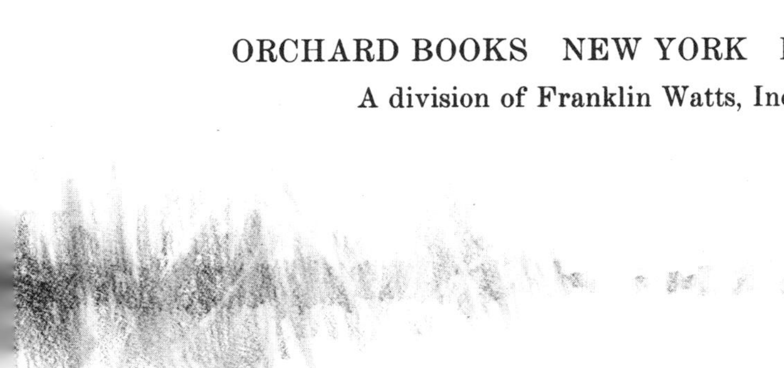

Orchard Books, 387 Park Avenue South
New York, New York 10016

Orchard Books Great Britain, 10 Golden Square
London W1R 3AF England

Orchard Books Australia, 14 Mars Road
Lane Cove, New South Wales 2066

Orchard Books Canada, 20 Torbay Road
Markham, Ontario 23P 1G6

Orchard Books is a division of Franklin Watts, Inc.

Manufactured in the United States of America
Book design by Mina Greenstein
The text of this book is set in 12 pt. Devinne.
The illustrations are pencil drawings reproduced in half-tone.

10 9 8 7 6 5 4 3 2

Library of Congress Cataloging-in-Publication Data
Lisle, Janet Taylor. The great Dimpole oak.
Summary: The citizens of Dimpole rally together to save an historic oak tree from being cut down.
[1. Trees—Fiction] I. Gammell, Stephen, ill. II. Title.
PZ7.L6912Gr 1987 [Fic] 87-11092
ISBN 0-531-05716-X ISBN 0-531-08316-0 (lib. bdg.)

The Great Dimpole Oak

VISIONS OF THE OAK

1

IT WAS A VERY OLD TREE. HOW OLD exactly? Well, that was one of its intriguing points—no one in Dimpole knew. There were theories. People had their stories. According to one, the tree was nearly a thousand years old and grew out of the place where a Viking raider once spat.

Some folks snorted at this. They said Dimpole was located fifty miles from the coast. They said Vikings had flat feet, which is why they took up sailing to begin with, and they never could have walked so far. These doubters believed in other stories about the oak's origins: It was planted by an Indian queen in 1492; it was planted by a groundhog in 1526; it was planted by a lightning bolt out of the blue. Or by wind. Or by flood. The infuriating thing about the oak was that with not much known for sure, all sorts of ideas came floating up around it. There was no way to tell what the real truth was.

Infuriating, yes, but what a magnificent tree! However the oak had started, it had grown up well. It was hundreds of feet tall, tens of feet thick, with roots as big as fire hoses coiled around its base. Everyone liked to sit on these roots and look out across the valley around Dimpole. Or they leaned back and gazed up, imagining shapes and faces in the ancient tangle of limbs overhead.

One root rose up and arched clear of the ground before plunging back into the soil. This the children rode, bucking and shrieking in the afternoons. But if a certain old farmer appeared, as he often did, they would stop riding for a while and listen to certain peculiar tales.

The Dimpole Oak was not located in the town of Dimpole but just outside, in the country. It grew in a hayfield that belonged to the farmer. He claimed ownership of the tree as well and he had his own ideas about it.

"This oak is a family tree," he explained to whoever would listen. "It was here when my great, great granddaddy came on the land. It'll still be here when my great, great grandchildren set foot in the world—which they haven't done yet by a long shot," he'd add, squinting up at the tree with a satisfied smile.

 According to the farmer, many strange events had occurred under his tree during the hundreds of years it had stood in the family field. His granddaddies had kept a record. They had passed the record down to each other, and then down to him, which was a good thing because otherwise the stories might have been lost, he said.

"Murder has been committed here," the farmer told the children of Dimpole in his gravelly voice. "And the blood of the victims has seeped down between these roots," he'd whisper, tapping his foot.

He told how thieves had plotted there, crouched together in winter moonlight. He described the criminals who had been hanged there and left to dry for days in the sun.

He recounted details of the famous Black Witches' Congress of 1685, when neighborhood cats were killed in cold blood and a young girl had disappeared. Sometimes, late at night, an eerie scream can be heard echoing across the fields, the farmer said. It might be a nighthawk or a cat on the prowl. It might be someone's nervous imagination. But it might be . . .

The old farmer would wink. "There's human blood in these branches and human sweat and human tears. It all came up the trunk, it did, from things that happened right here where I'm standing.

"And look here, look!" The farmer was always beckoning and whispering. "See all these carved hearts and lovers' initials? Some of them were cut more than three hundred years ago. It's peculiar when you think about it, isn't it? The carving's still here long after the real hearts were buried and rotted in the ground."

There were neighbors living nearby who did not like the farmer's stories. The way they saw it, the great oak was too noble and historic to be bogged down in a lot of grisly nonsense.

"Watch out for that farmer," they warned visitors who stopped to ask the way to the tree. "He's a crazy old fellow. He's got blood on the brain and half of what he says is a boldfaced lie."

Many of the farmer's neighbors had grown up with the oak. They believed it was just as much their tree as his. All the farmer's talk about his great granddaddy and grandchildren made them cross. Hadn't they ridden the tree's root when they were children? Hadn't they camped out under it and tried to climb up it and lived around it all their lives?

Moreover, they noted, the oak was history. And no one person can own history.

"That tree saw the British Red Coats march by on their way to a battle with the American colonists in 1775," said Mr. Harvey Glover one October day, down at the Dimpole Post Office. He was the town postmaster, a bird-like young man with darting eyes.

"That's right. A battle in which the Red Coats were defeated!" exclaimed plump Mrs. George Trawley, who came daily to pick up her mail. She smoothed down her bulges proudly at the thought of her country's victory.

"Did you know that our great President, Abraham Lincoln, stopped to sleep under our tree on a journey through these parts during the Civil War?" asked Miss Shirley Hand, an unusually pretty schoolteacher who lived in Dimpole. She handed the package she was carrying through the mail window to Mr. Glover and lowered her eyes sweetly.

"Is that true?" asked Mr. Glover. "I thought it was George Washington during the Revolution." Miss Hand had extremely long lashes, he noticed, as he reached for the rubber stamps.

"I'm glad to hear you say 'our tree,' " Mrs. Trawley told Miss Hand, "as there's some that would take every leaf and twig for themselves, never thinking of the rights of others."

Mr. Glover nodded. He leaned over the counter and spoke with hushed voice.

"The farmer is a sick man who ought to be in a hospital somewhere instead of wandering around scaring children with silly stories."

"Who's he been scaring?" asked Miss Hand. She smelled delightfully of lavender scent, Mr. Glover noticed. It happened to be his favorite perfume.

"Why, everybody!" he replied, more loudly than he had intended. "A child can't go up there to ride the root anymore without the old fellow scooting out from some bush and grabbing him."

"Grabbing him!" said Miss Hand with a horrified look.

"Well, ahem." Mr. Glover coughed. "Not grabbing exactly, but cornering. Then he tells his crazy stories about murder and hanging and branches full of blood. None of them are true, you know. He only does it to get attention."

"Not nice," murmured Mrs. Trawley. "Not nice at all. The little ones come home with their eyes popping out and the older ones get bad ideas."

"The poor things!" exclaimed Miss Hand. "I hadn't a notion this was going on."

"Not to mention . . ." Mr. Glover continued. (He shot an admiring glance toward Miss Hand's flushed cheeks.) "Not to mention the damage done to our tree's reputation. Why, left to the farmer, our great oak would become a lurid sideshow attracting the worst sort of people. Even now, there is no control over who comes to see the tree. He lets everybody in, for whatever reason."

"Something must be done," cried Miss Hand. "For the sake of the children!"

"A national treasure is in grave danger," agreed Mrs. Trawley.

"I will organize a meeting," Mr. Glover announced masterfully. "Before it is too late."

So, with a happy feeling that he had made a great impression on Miss Hand, Mr. Glover set to work compiling lists of names. He tracked down telephone numbers, bought note pads and sharpened pencils.

"None of which will do the least bit of good," Mrs. Trawley confided to Miss Hand later, in private. "Poor skinny Mr. Glover. He is not and never will be a leader of men."

Miss Hand was surprised to hear this. Mr. Glover had seemed perfectly nice to her. She was especially impressed by his concern for the children. But if Mrs. Trawley knew better . . .

Mrs. Trawley did know better. She happened to know the very person to organize a meeting of this sort. It was a person who had already made a name for herself by organizing everybody and everything in town.

"Why, who?" asked Miss Hand.

"Why, me," said Mrs. Trawley, fluffing herself up like a Thanksgiving turkey. "No one need worry about the farmer anymore. The Dimpole Oak is as good as saved. Mrs. George Trawley will arrange everything, and you will help her."

"I will?" said Miss Hand.

"Of course!"

At this, the women bent their heads together and began a long, serious conversation.

MISS HAND'S concern for the children ("the poor things") might have changed to alarm if she could have eavesdropped on a conversation taking place across town at that moment between two young Dimpolers.

Dexter Drake and Howlie Howlenburg were friends, next door neighbors and, more importantly, neighbors of the great oak as well. The boys were often among the farmer's visitors. They had heard the farmer's stories many times and they couldn't help feeling inspired by them.

Life certainly had been exciting back then in the past. By comparison, life in Dimpole these days had gotten so plain and ordinary that any normal adventurous person could go crazy sitting around and waiting for something to happen.

"And worse than crazy," Dexter was saying in an outraged voice to Howlie as the two walked home from school that October afternoon. "A person could get dumb and boring living around here. He could turn into a mouse."

"Well, not exactly," answered literal-minded Howlie.

"Listen," said Dexter. "When I grow up, I'm going to do things. I'm going to fight and plot and stab and rob and burn and ambush people if I have to, just like in the farmer's stories." He looked over at Howlie to see how he would take this. "And spit like a Viking," Dexter added, using a phrase well known in Dimpole and associated with strength and standing up for your rights. He cleared his throat and launched a huge glob of spit at a nearby bush.

Howlie cleared his throat and spat too.

"Sounds okay to me," he replied. "Too bad we have to wait till we're grown up." He hoisted his heavy book bag over his shoulder to keep it out of the dirt. Dexter, never one to bother about such things, was dragging his bag on the ground behind him.

"I've got five pages of fractions to do, eight vocabulary words to look up and a report due Friday on the herding habits of the wild Tibetan mountain goat," Howlie said. "What have you got?"

Instead of answering, Dexter staggered forward like a man on his last legs. He clutched his neck, wheezed, almost collapsed, caught himself at the last moment, nearly collapsed a second time and finally grabbed hold of Howlie for support. From this position, he cleared his throat again and shot a truly horrible glob in the direction of a fence post. Howlie stepped back to give him room.

"That was pretty good," he told Dexter. "It really looked as if you were about to die."

"Thanks," said Dexter. He let go of Howlie and straightened up with a pleased expression on his face.

"The trouble is," he said, continuing the original conversation, "you can do terrible things better and get away with them easier when you're old."

Howlie glanced at him. "Maybe you can," he said thoughtfully, "and then again, maybe not."

"What do you mean?"

"Well," said Howlie. "Who would ever suspect us, for instance, two ten-year-old kids who go to school every day . . ."

"And brush our teeth every night . . ." Dexter put in disgustedly.

"And have to clean out the garage . . ."

"And don't even get paid for it . . ."

"Who," said Howlie, "would ever suspect us of doing anything wild. I mean really wild."

"Nobody," muttered Dexter. "You're right. We're so wimpy we didn't even punch Bulldog Calhoun in the nose when he dropped that rock on my little sister's toe."

"We should have."

"I know it."

"He did it on purpose."

"He does things like that all the time."

"While we sit around and do nothing. Well, I'm tired of it," said Dexter. He jabbed his fist in the air. He wound up and did some complicated karate chops and leaps. Then without a pause he turned himself into Bulldog Calhoun getting punched and chopped to pieces. His head flew back. His stomach smashed in. His knees crumpled and he spat teeth.

Howlie stood back and watched in silence. When Dexter

had finished, he said: "You could probably be a stuntman in Hollywood with that stuff. It's starting to look realer and realer."

"Hollywood! Do you really think so?" exclaimed Dexter.

They were making their way down the long field that was home to the great oak. Up ahead, the tree loomed fiery-leaved against the cold, blue sky. The boys were in the habit of stopping by after school. There, if the farmer came out, they could listen to a story. And if he didn't come, that was all right too. They practiced riding the root or made up stories of their own. The Dimpole Oak had so many adventures connected to it that the air around it seemed like special air to Dexter and Howlie. It was exciting just to be there breathing.

But today, as they came up to it, the boys felt the old tree putting them to shame.

"We're in bad shape," Dexter told Howlie. "Are we mice or are we rats? It's time we did something. Something mean and tough. We've got to prove ourselves. We've got to show we're the kind of people other people don't fool around with."

"Especially Bulldog Calhoun."

"That oversized rat," Dexter growled. "Is it true that he chased you up a tree one time and said he would kill you with a stick if you came down and kept you there all day until you started crying?"

Howlie shot a horrified glance at his friend.

"Who told you that?"

Dexter shrugged. "Just heard it somewhere, I guess."

"Well, it's a lie," Howlie said, fiercely. "Nothing like that ever happened. How could anything like that happen? It's a dirty, rotten lie."

"Thought so," murmured Dexter, with his eyes turned away. "I never thought it was true."

"It isn't!" cried Howlie, "and that reminds me. Was that you I saw last Friday afternoon carrying a big bag of groceries out of the supermarket?"

Dexter's whole body jerked.

"Nah," he said. "It wasn't me."

Howlie shook his head. "I could've sworn it was you though I didn't see why you'd be carrying groceries out to Bulldog Calhoun's mother's car in the parking lot . . ."

"I wasn't!" Dexter broke in.

". . . while Bulldog walked ahead . . ."

"It wasn't me! Didn't I just say it wasn't?"

". . . with his hands in his pockets, kind of laughing to himself."

"He wasn't! He was not laughing!"

"Just thought I'd check," Howlie said. "It didn't look that much like you anyway."

The two fell silent again. They had reached the tree by now. They both looked up at it. Dexter sighed.

"We have got to do something fast," he said.

 Howlie nodded. The boys dropped to their knees and

put their heads close together. They each picked up a twig and cleared some grass out from between the tree's roots to make a dirt drawing board. There they plotted until dusk, glancing over their shoulders at times and straightening up to shoot defiant wads of spit at the tree's trunk.

The farmer spied them from his window, but he didn't go out that day to join them. Despite his blustery manner with visitors, the farmer wasn't a strong man anymore. He was prone, from the years of hard work he'd put into his farm, to creaks and aches, especially about the knees. That day, he sat on his living room couch with his legs propped up on the coffee table and looked out the window.

What are those boys up to? the farmer thought to himself. He might have asked the question out loud if there had been somebody in the house to answer him. Unfortunately, he lived alone. His wife had died, and his children were grown and lived with their children in distant cities.

What was it the boys reminded him of, the farmer wondered, crouched down that way, two little shadows under the monumental shadow of the Dimpole Oak, and evening coming on and the bats beginning to flicker?

They reminded him of a story. It was a story about two pirates, who buried a chest of diamonds at the foot of the tree and then murdered each other in a bloody fit of greed.

This was the kind of story two boys ought to hear, the lonely farmer thought. They ought to learn about greed. They should know about the buried diamonds. He half rose from his couch to go outside and tell them.

Just then, a red moon crested the darkening horizon. Far away, a hawk screamed. The wind outside the house seemed suddenly full of whispers. Or was this only the imagination of the old man?

It is true that his head had drooped back against
the sofa cushions and that the spurt
of a snore could be heard
from deep down in
his throat.

WHILE the farmer slept and dreamt about old stories, another vivid imagination was homing in on the great oak from an entirely different direction.

In a cave somewhere north of Bombay, India, a wise and learned swami was just completing a series of difficult calculations.

These calculations, which had already taken two years of work, concerned holiness. In particular, the swami wanted to find out which places on earth were holiest, which places were next holy, which came next and so on down the line to the most low-down and spiritless areas. The swami planned to use this information to map out his upcoming world tour, avoiding the spiritless areas, where he never looked his best.

The swami's calculations took place entirely inside his head. For months he had sat motionless in the doorway of his cave, showing no more sign of his labor than an occasional puff of smoke out the right ear.

His face was blank. His eyes were turned in. His hands lay furled and forgotten in his lap. Under his turban, however, his brain sparked, hissed and ran at a high rate of speed. Great plains of human knowledge were crossed, steep cliffs were scaled, canyons were probed, and dead ends were averted with screeching, last-second turns that left streaks of hot rubber in their wake.

It was following one of these hair-raising turns that the

swami's mind suddenly jumped its track and crashed headlong into the ghostly figure of what appeared to be an enormous oak tree.

Outside, the swami did not bat an eye. Inside, his mind spun around twice, saw stars and finally lifted itself to its elbows (so to speak) to peer at the object before him.

It was a tree, all right. And unless the swami's five-hundred horsepower intelligence was mistaken, this tree had an unusually large amount of holiness packed into its trunk. Deep red waves of holy current poured from crevices in its bark, and every twig was surrounded by a paler, but no less amazing, crimson halo.

The tree dazzled the swami's inner eye. It was beautiful. It was elegant. Its bark was a soft gray color. Its long branches swept the ground. A fleeting aroma of—what was it? lavender perhaps?—rose to the swami's nostrils. Temporarily, he swooned.

Several hours passed before the holy man could begin work on the practical aspects of his discovery. Even then, his progress was slow. After a great struggle with the tree's powerful red current, he managed to compute the oak's longitude and latitude. He measured its height and breadth, its age, the average length of its branches and, in a bonus rush of brilliance, conjured up the picture of a tall, bony, bearded man in a black top hat lying asleep under the tree while a crowd of people gathered nearby

 whispering such words as:

"Look! Our President!"

"That oversized rat. Did you hear his last speech?"

"Well, I think he's wonderful."

"Well, I think he's weak-kneed."

"He's a devoted father."

"He's a sick man and ought to be in a hospital somewhere."

The swami could make sense of none of this, so he returned to his measuring and calculating.

At length, the swami figured the voltage of the oak tree's extraordinary red current to be the greatest and holiest on earth. With this information, and by now practically leaping with joy, he decided to visit the tree immediately. He therefore began the difficult (and rather nauseating) process of rising out of himself. He swiveled his inward eyes outward. He pried his hands open. He took control again of his facial expressions: mouth curved down wisely, nostrils flared nobly, eyebrows furrowed patiently.

When he had done these things, he stood up out of his two-year crouch (but how thin his legs had become!) and teetered off down a mountain path to inform his loyal followers, who were camped in a lower-level cave, of the great expedition that lay before them.

2

"WISK-BUZZ-SLAP! WISK-BUZZ-SLAP!

What was that strange noise?

"Wisk-buzz-SLAP!"

Was it someone chasing flies with a fly swatter? No.

Was it a small twin-engine airplane whose fuel lines had clogged in midair? The engines wouldn't start! The plane was falling!

No.

"Wisk-buzz-SLAP!"

Was it a giant, flat-footed Viking walking down the middle of Main Street, planting oak trees left and right?

No, no. What an imagination!

 It was only Mr. Glover's xerox machine hard at work in

the back room at the post office. While Mr. Glover dozed and dreamed in his chair, the machine was turning out—"Wisk-buzz-SLAP!"—hundreds of bright red leaflets announcing the coming of Great Dimpole Oak Day, on Saturday, October 25th, 9 a.m. to 4 p.m.

"Rally round one and all,
Or the great tree will fall."

The idea for Great Dimpole Oak Day had come from Mrs. Trawley.

"We must raise enthusiasm for our tree. And money," she said at a meeting that she and Mr. Glover called not long after their first conversation in the post office.

"Great Dimpole Oak Day will be a chance for families and friends to come together to celebrate history. I will give a speech," Mrs. Trawley announced. "In addition, we will have balloons, games, refreshments, and perhaps some Special Entertainment."

Mrs. Trawley had taken the project rather into her own hands, Mr. Glover couldn't help noticing. It was she who had written the threatening jingle about the great oak falling—soon to be distributed far and wide, to her great satisfaction.

"Not that a tree that size is in any danger of actually falling," Mr. Glover pointed out a little peckishly.

"I was thinking of it falling into the wrong hands," Mrs. Trawley replied. She gave him a piercing look.

"I see," said Mr. Glover through tightened lips.

"I was thinking of the farmer," Mrs. Trawley told him impatiently. "That boastful farmer who has given our tree such a bad name."

"And terrified our children," said Miss Hand, who was also present at the meeting.

"The farmer believes our oak to be his personal family heirloom, can you imagine?" Mrs. Trawley added in disgust. "I will never understand the bull-headedness of some people."

"What kind of Special Entertainment did you have in mind?" asked Miss Hand. She had just had a vision of a matador with a red cape and the farmer on all fours charging madly around a Spanish bullring. "Were you thinking of music, dancing, a magician . . . ?" She trailed off doubtfully.

"My dear, I leave that entirely up to you," said Mrs. Trawley, organizing ruthlessly.

"Me!"

"I'm sure with your quick, young brain you will think of something."

And, although Miss Hand was not sure she would think of anything (even if she had time to think, which, with all the hours she spent teaching, she usually did not have), Mrs. Trawley slipped like a greased pig to the next order of business. This concerned the monument to be erected at the base of the great oak.

 "Monument!" exclaimed Mr. Glover, lurching forward

in surprise. "I should think the tree is monumental enough in its own right."

"Well, we could have a memorial plaque screwed into the bark," Mrs. Trawley conceded. "But we must have something to remind us of exactly what the great oak stands for."

"Which is?" Mr. Glover's feathers were ruffled. Ordinarily, he would not have asked such a question. If only Mrs. Trawley didn't feel that she had to climb into every driver's seat in sight!

"The oak stands for liberty, equality and Abraham Lincoln resting in peace," interjected Miss Hand. "Its roots made a pillow for a great head."

"I can take issue there!" Mr. Glover cried. "George Washington's head is the only great head that has passed beneath the oak. I have checked the town records. And he did not do anything so foolish as to doze off in plain view of everyone. He rode underneath, proud in his saddle, and it is said that his eyes traveled up the massive trunk and that he nodded as he passed, in the way a great warrior might nod to greet and acknowledge an equal greatness."

Mr. Glover glanced triumphantly at Miss Hand, whom he suspected of secretly admiring him. Then he looked at Mrs. Trawley. The fat woman shook her head.

"My dear Mr. Glover. How could we raise a monument to something so small and unnoticeable as a nod? And surely Miss Hand is right. I myself remember learning in school all about President Lincoln's noble sleep; how he drew strength and courage from our tree, and rode forth with a new plan to save the nation."

"That is unfounded rumor," snapped Mr. Glover.

"My own idea," Mrs. Trawley went on, "is for a cast bronze monument. It would show the weary figure of Lincoln laid down, cradled, if you like, at the foot of our tree, the mother oak."

Miss Hand nodded eagerly.

"Mother oak!" screeched Mr. Glover. "You want to turn our old warrior of a tree into a defenseless mother? And reduce a great man to a gurgling baby? What on earth would Lincoln say? And poor George Washington. He would weep if he could see his magnificent nod fallen so low, and in diapers no less. Mother oak! That must never be!

"Why, she is mad," Mr. Glover said, speaking toward Miss Hand with a hopeful look. He glared at Mrs. Trawley. "You are mad and should be taken to a hospital before it's too . . ."

"I see we have a small difference of opinion," Mrs. Trawley interrupted, icily. She licked her lips and knotted her right fist into a threatening lump.

"Wisk-buzz-CRUNCH!"

Mr. Glover woke suddenly from his nap in the back room at the post office and found, with relief, that he had only been dreaming. Mrs. Trawley was not really about to punch him in the nose. Still, as is often the case with dreams, much of Mr. Glover's dream was true. He was just beginning to wonder what part of it was real and what part he had merely dreamed when . . .

"Wisk-buzz-CRUNCH!" It came again. "What is that awful noise?" said Mr. Glover, leaping to his feet.

His eyes fell upon his xerox machine, which seemed to have stopped working. A thin tendril of smoke rose from what might have been the machine's right ear, if it had had one. (Mr. Glover's copier had a weirdly human look around its control panel, especially a pair of small, green eyes that seemed to glow almost evilly at times.)

Now, at last, Mr. Glover understood the meaning of the scene before him. Hundreds, perhaps thousands, of red leaflets lay at his feet, shredded beyond recognition. Something terrible had happened to the xerox machine. Strips of paper dangled from its slot-like mouth. One green eye was out while the other blinked mindlessly, like a broken traffic light.

"Idiot machine!" shouted Mr. Glover. He slumped in his chair. The bulky figure of Mrs. Trawley loomed before his inner eye: "I suppose you can do the xeroxing," she had told him. "Xeroxing is not very difficult."

Mr. Glover sighed. More annoying still, he began to see how Abraham Lincoln, carrying the problems of a nation on his shoulders, might have succumbed to sleep beneath the Dimpole Oak.

Mr. Glover felt his head sag back against the chair

cushions. He looked up to where a complicated network of plaster cracks branched and sub-branched across the ceiling. He shut his eyes against all problems and tormentors—even the delightful Miss Hand—and dropped into a deep slumber.

WHILE Mr. Glover and his xerox machine snoozed side by side at the post office, half-buried in scarlet shreds, another pair of conspirators were wallowing in another red heap several miles away.

Under the Dimpole Oak, submerged in a pile of fallen leaves, Dexter Drake and Howlie Howlenburg looked at each other unhappily. A week had passed since they had sworn to take action against the bully, Bulldog Calhoun. So far, they hadn't been able to think of any plans. The trouble was Bulldog himself, who was so mean and crafty that any ordinary plan looked weak beside him. The boys were forced to consider acts of evil far beyond their abilities.

"We could bury him alive," Dexter had suggested.

"But then we'd need equipment. Shovels, air hoses, food and water, rope to tie him up with and handkerchiefs to stuff down his throat," sensible Howlie pointed out. "Besides that, we'd have to find a box big enough to put him in. Or build one. Have you ever tried to build a box? It's not easy."

"We could poison him," Dexter had gone on. "You know, inject an orange with cyanide solution and put it in his lunch box."

To illustrate this idea, Dexter picked an orange out of thin air. He peeled it, divided the fruit into four parts, placed a quarter in his mouth and chewed. Then, with a single dramatic retch, he keeled over and died. Howlie applauded.

"Or we could scalp him," Dexter went on, when he came to. "We could stick his feet in a tub of wet cement and . . ."

But all these ideas were clearly beyond the scope of two ten-year-old boys, even boys fired up by the oak tree's long and unwholesome history.

"How about asking the farmer?" Howlie said, on this day of the leaf pile. "He's got stacks of gruesome ideas stored away."

Dexter looked across the field and up toward the old man's house. As on most days recently, they had the tree to themselves. The weather had turned raw and cold. Whether because of this or some more personal reason, the farmer kept indoors. Occasionally, they caught sight of his shape standing at a living room window. Perhaps he was feeling gloomy about how few children came to play under the tree in such weather.

It seemed to Dexter that the farmer had grown older and shakier this year. His eightieth birthday was almost upon him, it was said. Lately, he'd taken to clutching people's shoulders when he told his wild tales, as if he were afraid they might run away from him.

"I don't know about you," Dexter told Howlie, "but I got kind of tired of the farmer's stories this summer. Four times in one month, he told the one about the two greedy pirates stabbing each other to death at the foot of the tree.

And every time he thought he was telling a brand new story he'd just remembered."

Howlie nodded.

"And all those things about the tree having special powers and human blood in its branches, I used to believe them but I don't anymore," Dexter continued. "You get to a certain age and you just can't believe things like that."

"I know," said Howlie.

"It's dangerous, I mean. People would laugh at you," Dexter said. "You've got to know the difference between what's real and what's made up or people will think you're strange."

"Or sick in the head," Howlie agreed, tapping his forehead.

"Or stupid," said Dexter. He stopped and snapped his fingers. "Wait a minute. That gives me an idea."

"What?" cried Howlie.

"We'll be pirates. We'll fight each other with knives. We'll circle each other slowly and greedily, then we'll reach out and stab each other right through our hearts."

Howlie gazed at his friend in horror.

"Stab each other? But why?"

Dexter crowed with delight. "For Bulldog Calhoun! Don't you see? He knows the story about the pirates and their chest of diamonds as well as we do. He's heard it from the farmer twenty times, just like us."

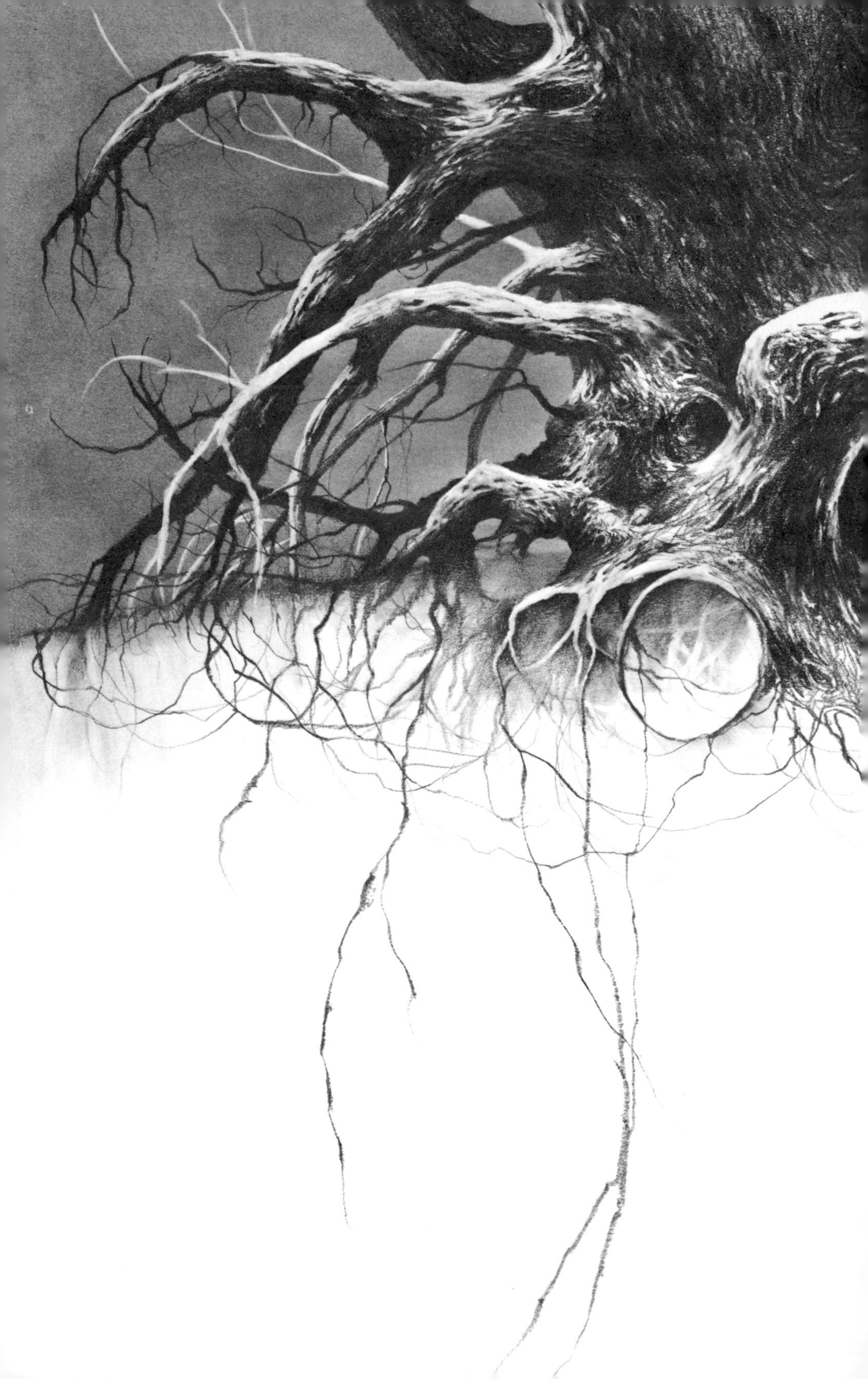

"And he's never believed it," Howlie said. "We don't believe it either—we were just saying so."

"So what? We're going to show him how it could have happened. We'll fight to the death right before his eyes. Not for real, of course," Dexter added, seeing the alarm on Howlie's face. "We'll fake it. Bulldog will think it's real, though."

Howlie shook his head. "Listen, Dexter," he said. "You're good at acting out things like that. You're brilliant, in fact. But I'm not. How could I pretend I'm dead? For that matter, how could I kill you?"

"Anybody who tries can pretend to be dead," Dexter said. "And there's some red paint in my garage. I saw it when we cleaned the place up last time."

"Red paint! What for?"

"Blood," said Dexter, coolly. "Isn't there a way of making it spurt out when we need it? Come on, Howlie. That's your department."

"Well, there's plastic bags," Howlie answered reluctantly.

"Plastic bags?"

"That's how they do it when they need blood on the stage. They pour the stuff into a plastic bag, seal it up and hide it under their shirts. Then, when they need to bleed, they stick a hole in the bag. I read all about it."

"Well? Couldn't we do that?" said Dexter. "We could stab each other's plastic bags. Let's do it! Let's do it this Saturday."

"What will Bulldog do when he thinks we're killed?" Howlie asked.

"He'll scream and run like a scared cat," Dexter replied. "Or maybe he'll pass out. Whatever he does, he'll look stupid, especially when we come back to life without a scratch on us. We might even decide to haunt him for a few days."

"Maybe he'll cry," whispered Howlie.

"Cry!" Dexter whispered back. "Oh, great. Great!"

The friends grabbed each other and began to dance in the leaf pile, with shrieks and leaps that sent up leaves like volcanic eruptions.

"WHAT ARE those boys up to?" Mrs. Trawley murmured to herself as she maneuvered her enormous car over to the side of the road and stopped. She had been passing by the historic oak tree on her way up the road to deliver leaflets for Great Dimpole Oak Day when her eye had fallen on the frenzied dance.

"Here! Boys!" Mrs. Trawley called out the car window. "Stop that at once and come away from there. That's right. Come here. You'll just get into trouble in this place.

"What on earth were you doing?" asked Mrs. Trawley when the two came up to the car, somewhat shamefaced. "In you get," she added, opening the back door with one of her long, fleshy arms. "You can help me deliver these leaflets. One to each mailbox. They're to announce Great

Dimpole Oak Day next Saturday. You'll want to come yourselves. It will be such fun. Games. Lemonade. I am giving a speech. Mr. Glover is a helpless fool. I've had to do everything myself, even print up these announcements. Do you know I found him asleep in the post office this afternoon? And all his leaflets were ruined."

Mrs. Trawley chatted on but, sitting side by side in the back seat, Dexter and Howlie didn't hear a word. They were catching each other's eye and grinning wickedly.

Once, Howlie pulled out an invisible knife and pretended to stab it into Dexter's heart. This sent them off into gales of hysterical—though absolutely silent—laughter.

THE MORNING SUN was just rising, hot as a bowl of Indian curry, when the swami set off downhill for Bombay with his loyal followers, thirty strong, and an assortment of goats and peacocks.

The swami was in a bad humor. He had not slept well the night before. He had tossed and scratched on his bed of nails. He had thought about the great oak and he had thought about himself. He had come to certain uncomfortable realizations.

The swami was a failure—oh yes! He saw it very clearly. He had meditated too long and done too little in his life. He had thought himself powerful, had prided himself on his intelligence and self-discipline. Alas! The great oak had shown him. Measured beside the tree, the swami now saw how pitiful and insignificant he was. His holiness was a drop in the bucket beside the tree's immense lake. How brief was his life compared to the oak's, how thin his skin, how short his root.

"This is terrible!" the swami cried out to himself as he wound down the treacherous mountain path. "I must improve. I must change."

By the time he had reached the Bombay city limits he was gritting his teeth and pounding his turban in anguish. Just then he caught sight of his loyal followers, a dirty band loping behind him in dogged silence. The swami shook his fist at them. Why were they always at his heels?

"Away! Go away!" he cried. "I cannot be your leader anymore."

The band would not be driven off. With maddening stillness it kept pace.

"Be gone!" called the swami. "I am no longer what I was. I must begin again. I must work. You must all return to your homes."

But the followers did not go. If they had once had homes, they seemed now to have forgotten the way back. When the swami turned and glared at them, they shuffled their feet and pretended to examine their long, ragged fingernails.

What a sight they made, slouching about in smoky rabbit hides, moss dangling from their eyebrows, vegetable juice on their chins. The swami was disgusted by them. He felt ashamed to be seen with such a band. The swami looked back at the hills down which they had walked and wondered how he had managed not to notice it before. His loyal followers were a wreck. All their outdoor living had taken a toll. While the swami's spirit had soared and purified itself on high, his followers had starved, frozen, thirsted and broiled down below. Their skins had dried up, their stomachs had caved in, and now—look at them!

The swami shook his head slowly at the thirty ravaged faces that watched him with uncomplaining misery. Uncomplaining, yes. The swami's expression softened.

 "Come," he murmured to them. He opened his arms and

gestured for them to come near him. The followers cowered like whipped dogs.

"Come closer," the swami said, kindly. "I have good news. We are all going to a shop to buy new clothes."

The whipped dogs eyed him unbelievingly.

"Then we will all go to my apartment in Bombay, to take showers and cut our nails and snip the moss from our hair."

Apartment in Bombay? The dogs had never heard of such a thing. They glanced in alarm at their hands.

"After that," the swami went on, patting the shoulder of the nearest follower, "we are all going out to dinner at a very expensive restaurant to fortify ourselves for the trip ahead. We will order anything on the menu that we want: mango ice cream, tandoori shrimp, even chicken livers with red-hot spices."

At the mention of this last, the swami's loyal followers surged a bit and licked their lips hungrily. They could not quite remember what an expensive restaurant was, but were prepared as usual to follow the swami's lead.

"And after that we will get in an airplane!" cried the swami, leaping down the street, completely carried away by his own generosity. Clearly, he was beginning to change and improve already. "And we will fly first class, nonstop, to the United States, to find this most wonderful tree. My oak tree, the one I discovered."

The loyal followers nodded eagerly.

"It is a tree of the most amazing power," the swami explained, dabbing at his eyes with a banyan leaf. Suddenly, he was overcome by emotion. "Greater than my power by a thousand times, oh yes."

He blew his nose loudly into the leaf. His followers hung their heads.

"And why," the swami went on, sniffling, "why this tree should have chosen to grow so far away from us, in a foreign country, among strangers who cannot see its meaning, I do not know. Life is mysterious indeed. Do you suppose it was to test us?"

The followers muttered a group answer that could have been either yes or no.

"Come along then," the swami said, for he had spied a handsome-looking clothing store just opening for the day's business across the street. The followers crossed behind him and entered the shop in a shy cluster that reeked of goats and outdoor cooking.

IT WAS 9:15 in the morning when the swami approached a salesman and began to order new sandals and clothing for himself and his followers.

At the same moment in Dimpole, it was quite late at night, and people who were still awake were switching on the 11 o'clock news or whistling their dogs in from outside. This is because ten hours always separate Dimpole and Bombay on the clock, with Bombay coming in front.

In Dimpole, those bloodthirsty schemers Dexter Drake and Howlie Howlenburg had long since gone to sleep in their beds. ("How angelic! How dear!" murmured their mothers, looking in on them with gentle smiles.)

Seated at her dressing table, Mrs. Trawley was rolling her hair onto foam rubber curlers and eating jelly beans out of her bathrobe pocket.

"Four score and seven years ago, our forefathers brought forth on this continent a new nation," Mrs. Trawley recited to herself between munches. "Conceived in liberty and dedicated to the proposition that (munch, munch)."

Mrs. Trawley was nervous about the speech she was scheduled to give on Great Dimpole Oak Day. What should she say? There is nothing like a quick run-through of the Gettysburg Address to start the juices flowing, she thought, as she reached for another jelly bean.

Mr. Glover and Miss Hand were in bed reading mystery stories. (Not in the same bed, or in the same house.) They both loved mystery stories, and always read them before going to sleep. Neither knew of the other's habit, however. Reading in bed is not usually a subject you can discuss with someone until you know him a little better than over a post office counter.

The farmer stood stiffly at his living room window, which was open a crack. Away in the field, the oak waved its branches in an evening breeze. The farmer could not actually see the tree because it was engulfed by night. But he knew it was there, waving at him.

The farmer had lived on the farm for so long that he no longer needed to see its parts. He could just as easily cross one of his fields in his mind as on foot. He could open the barn door, go inside, look around, smell the fresh hay, listen to the swallows nesting under the eaves, all as if it were really happening—only it would be happening in the barn of his head instead of out in the real barn.

The farmer gazed out the dark window with an amused look on his face. How convenient it was to walk around this way, he thought. For a person with bad knees, it was the best way to travel. Darkness could not stop him. Neither could bad weather. He could go wherever he wanted, leaving whenever he wished.

Tromp, tromp, tromp. The farmer walked out under the oak tree and stood there listening. What did he hear?

 Memories, of course. The farmer heard flocks of memories rustling overhead, just as if they were real birds stopping by on their trip south for the winter. Like the real birds, the memories flashed bright and cocky before his eyes, then flew back to perches above him in the oak.

Flash: There was his wife, Ellen, working in the garden up the hill. He saw the familiar blue of the kerchief she always wore over her hair.

"Hello!" she cried down to him, and waved. "These flowers are in a terrible state. All weeds and vines!"

Flash: He saw himself as a strong, hardworking young farmer in overalls, coming out the back door early in the morning, rolling up his sleeves. He closed the back door softly because the children were still asleep inside. There was a whole list of things he had to do but he took time to close the door, quiet as a mouse.

Flash: The farmer saw himself again, as a boy this time, blond, skinny, with a fancy new birthday jackknife slung from his belt. He walked around the old oak with it, tough and grown-up. He took the knife off his belt and carved his name in the tree. Just three letters, "Bob," but he managed to give his hand a good slice. He ran back to the house spouting blood.

"He's too young for that knife," his mother said. "See what happened?"

His father said: "Yes, but he'll learn."

Well, he certainly had learned. At the living room window, the farmer drew a wrinkled, white handkerchief from his back pocket. He blew his nose and wiped his eyes. The knife was long lost, but the memory of himself on his tenth birthday all those years ago touched his deepest feelings. He was too young then: now he was too old.

In the darkness outside the window, the oak moved its branches in a breeze. When the farmer heard the familiar rustling sound his eyes filled with tears a second time—he could not think why—and he had to blow his nose all over again and dab at himself like a sentimental old lady.

To pull himself together—Who would have thought that a man nearly eighty years old could be swept by such currents?—the farmer did a small mathematical calculation on his fingers. He counted, and reckoned that there were five days left before his birthday.

"Five days!" he muttered. "Until October 25th . . . Next Saturday," he added, to clear it up in his mind.

By now it was midnight, but the farmer suddenly decided that he must write a letter to his grandchildren. He sat at his desk, took a sheet of paper from a drawer, and began. His handwriting had become so shaky lately that he hardly recognized it himself.

In the letter, the farmer did not mention his upcoming birthday. He wrote about the birds migrating south for the winter, about the brilliant red of the oak's leaves. (*Like a setting sun,* he said.)

He wrote to his grandchildren about the two small boys he had seen under the oak, and how they reminded him of himself when he was a boy. Then he signed off abruptly: *Love from your Grandpa,* with a rather worse scrawl than usual.

The farmer put the letter in an envelope and, in spite of the late hour, he carried it out to the mailbox at the end of his driveway. Afterwards, he walked slowly back to the house and went upstairs to bed.

Would his grandchildren remember a birthday they had often forgotten in the past, a birthday that the farmer was too shy to remind them of? Would they come from the city to give him a party? Would they jump suddenly through the front door with balloons and presents and an eighty-candle birthday cake?

A surprise party! The farmer's eyes lit up when he thought of it. Of course! he thought, as he brushed his old yellow teeth. That was why his grandchildren had not called or written to him recently. They were pretending to ignore him. They were pretending to forget all about him so that he would be doubly surprised on his birthday.

"How clever. A surprise party," the farmer murmured happily. He sat on the bed in his pajamas and pulled his stiff legs one by one off the floor.

When he had laid them straight, he covered them with blankets and lay back himself.

3

THE FARMER WAS NOT THE ONLY one counting on his fingers during the week before Saturday, October 25th. Down at the post office, Mrs. Trawley counted up to three on the little sausages of her left hand. She shook the hand under Mr. Glover's nose.

"Have you bought the paper cups yet?" she demanded. "Have you ordered the hot dogs? Where are the balloons? Do you realize that Great Dimpole Oak Day will be here in three days? Three days!" Mrs. Trawley cried. "And where are the screws for the brass plaque?"

Mr. Glover glared at her. He had the screws in his pocket but decided not to tell. He did not appreciate being spoken to like a whipped dog.

Mrs. Trawley hardly noticed. She did not expect answers to any of the questions she had just asked. Mr. Glover was a spindly sparrow of a person. He had no sense of how to order people around and get things done. Why, if it had been left to him, the Dimpole Oak would most likely have been sold as a hamburger stand by now, while the farmer cruised the Mediterranean on his ill-gotten gains.

Luckily, Mrs. Trawley had stepped in to save the day. She had organized everyone in town, as usual. It was no use hiding from her, as Mr. Higgins, owner and manager of H. Higgins' Dimpole Grocery, had discovered.

"Harold Higgins! You come up out of that apple cellar this minute!" Mrs. Trawley had called from the top of the store's cellar stairs. Below her, all was dark and silent.

"I know you're down there. I know you don't want to see me. But here I am and I need free napkins and free soda for my rally at the oak tree on Saturday. If you can't come up and hand them over like a man, I'm sure your wife would like to know where you were instead of fishing a week ago last Wednesday night. . . ."

"Harry Higgins has kindly offered us twenty cases of cola, twenty cases of orange soda, and ice," Mrs. Trawley told Mr. Glover now, in the post office. "He has said he will deliver them personally to the tree on Saturday morning. Now *there* is a man of action."

"Hah!" said Mr. Glover.

"Hah yourself."

Mrs. Trawley certainly did not have time to stand

around talking to useless post office clerks. She had a hundred details to attend to. For one thing, the bronze statue of Abraham Lincoln asleep had proved too difficult to arrange on such short notice. She had been forced back upon the memorial plaque, and there were all sorts of problems with it, as there always are with plaques.

"Of course you don't know anything about plaques," Mrs. Trawley told Mr. Glover crossly. She sailed out of the post office, calling back over her shoulder:

"Did you hear? We are planning a march. We will march on the tree carrying signs and flags at 9 a.m. on Saturday. That will show the old farmer how the town of Dimpole feels. Everybody is coming!"

A march! Mr. Glover snorted. In the back room, he gave the broken xerox machine a nasty kick and watched with satisfaction as its second green eye quivered and went dead.

What was it about the xerox machine that reminded Mr. Glover of Mrs. Trawley? There was a resemblance, no doubt about it. The gaping mouth, perhaps? A few shreds of red leaflet still hung from the machine's slot, looking rather like strands of spaghetti. Was Mrs. Trawley fond of eating spaghetti? Somehow, Mr. Glover suspected she was. Now that he thought about it, he could imagine her gobbling huge plates of spaghetti and dangling the noodles messily down her chin.

Mr. Glover gave the xerox machine another kick.

 "A monster of a woman," he was muttering, "a perfect

gobbler of a . . ."—when he heard the front door of the post office open. He peeked around the corner to see who had come in.

"Miss Hand!"

"Mr. Glover. Hello."

"Well . . . Well . . . I . . . this is a surprise," stammered Mr. Glover.

"I've come to buy stamps," Miss Hand replied with lowered eyes. "I found I was all out of stamps last night and I thought . . ."

She began to rummage in her purse. She was wearing a dress of the most delicious pink. Mr. Glover moved up behind the counter and looked on.

"And I thought," Miss Hand continued, groping more frantically, "I thought to myself: 'I simply must buy stamps. Bright and early tomorrow morning. Before school. Stamps cannot wait.' "

A noise that sounded like a large pile of gravel shifting position came from inside the purse. Mr. Glover leaned forward over the counter. What did women carry in their purses? he wondered. It was an ongoing mystery, for he had always been too shy to ask.

"Stamps will not wait!" said Miss Hand, burrowing deeper, "but must be bought without delay as soon as can be. One cannot go on long without stamps."

With a final lunge into the purse she came up with a brown leather wallet.

"Oh!" exclaimed Mr. Glover, stepping back.

Miss Hand looked up at him from under her long lashes. "I always know it's hiding in there somewhere," she said.

Mr. Glover did not know what to say to this. He looked away in confusion and began to take out sheets of stamps from a drawer.

"Do you have the stamps with the seashells on them?" Miss Hand asked, leaning over the counter to look for herself. A rush of lavender scent came with her. Mr. Glover felt thoroughly light-headed.

"Oh! You have a new one," Miss Hand said. "Calico Scallop. I already have the New England Neptune and the Lightning Whelk at home. I have heard there is a beauty called 'Reticulated Helmet.' Have you heard of it by any chance?"

Mr. Glover had not only heard of it, he happened to have this very stamp not two feet away in a drawer. Miss Hand was very impressed. She had been a little afraid of Mr. Glover in the past, and had decided to visit the post office this morning only after much soul-searching. He had seemed so snappish at times. But today—Miss Hand smiled in his direction—today he was positively charming. And despite Mrs. Trawley's warning, he appeared extremely well-organized, even if he wasn't a leader of men. Miss Hand was not sure she would have gotten on very well with a full-fledged leader of men anyway. She disliked being told to do things.

"I read a mystery story once about a woman who collected seashells and kept them in a special room on long racks of sand," she told Mr. Glover to keep the conversation going. "But it was a cover-up, of course. Buried under the shells were the bodies of all her dead husbands. The police found them at the end in a most gruesome chapter."

Mr. Glover did not seem at all disturbed by this scenario.

"Oh! Do you read mysteries?" he asked. "They're my favorite kind of book."

From here, the conversation might have taken off with lightning speed but for Miss Hand's discovery that she was already five minutes late for her class. The children would be standing on their heads in the hall by the time she arrived. She hurried out of the post office to her car.

"See you on Saturday," Mr. Glover called after her.

"Saturday?"

"It's Great Dimpole Oak Day, remember?"

"Oh, dear. So it is. And I have promised Mrs. Trawley to come up with a Special Entertainment. It's far too late now to think of anything. What shall I do?" Miss Hand got into her car and slammed the door hard after herself.

"Don't worry about that woman," Mr. Glover called to her over the roar of the motor. "She is a menace to society. But . . . would you consider marching to the tree with me on Saturday morning?"

"What? What? Marching to the sea?" Miss Hand shouted back, cupping her ear. Her old sedan was making a terrible racket.

"To the tree!" yelled Mr. Glover. "Marching . . . to . . . the . . . *tree!*"

Miss Hand was still not sure she had heard correctly, but she felt embarrassed to go on shouting. She smiled and waved and accelerated quickly out of the post office parking lot.

"Marching to the sea?" she murmured to herself. An image of lemmings galloping insanely toward the edge of a sandy cliff rose before her. But that, certainly, was not what nice Mr. Glover had meant. . . .

DEXTER DRAKE and Howlie Howlenburg did not have Miss Hand as their teacher. Miss Hand taught the second grade at Dimpole School. Dexter and Howlie were in the fifth grade, and their teacher was not the sort of woman to dazzle the eye of a man like Mr. Glover. She was a powerfully built person named Miss Matterhorn who never wore perfume and was never late to class.

Even as Mr. Glover slid back (with thumping heart) behind his counter in the post office, Dexter and Howlie were hard at work on a sheet of math problems. By the time Miss Hand arrived to take charge of her second graders, the boys had moved on to the worse misery of vocabulary notebooks.

From her desk at the back of the room, Miss Matterhorn kept watch, tapping her pencil on the blotter at intervals. She had heard rumors that her students didn't like her. But why? She was such a nice person. From the back of the room, Miss Matterhorn had been trying to detect the answer for years. Unfortunately, her eyesight was terrible.

Howlie: Dexter wrote in the note he dropped on Howlie's desk when he got up to sharpen his pencil—*What do you think we should tell Bulldog Calhoun to make him come to the oak tree at dawn this Saturday?*

When Howlie got up to fetch more scratch paper, he dropped an answer. *Dexter: Why does it have to be dawn? Bulldog will never come then. He hates getting up in the morning.*

Dexter asked for permission to go to the bathroom. On the way to the door, he pitched a pencil onto Howlie's desk. There was a note wrapped around it. It said:

Howlie: Dawn is when the pirates in the farmer's story fought each other to death. It's the best time to fight. Everybody always fights at dawn.

When Dexter came past Howlie's desk on the way back from the bathroom, Howlie handed him a ballpoint pen. Inside, there was a rolled-up message.

Dexter: How about telling Bulldog that we've found the buried diamonds from the farmer's story? Bulldog loves money. He might believe it. Anyway, people do find old treasure sometimes.

This note stirred Dexter to a new level of interest.

Holy cow! Do you think there really could be a chest of diamonds? he wrote back. *Has anyone ever tried digging around the tree?* Feeling the press of time, Dexter shot this note to Howlie by glider.

Not that I know of. (Howlie, also by glider.)

Maybe the farmer's story is true!!! (Dexter, glider.)

Probably not. (Howlie, return flight.)

But this could be one of the strange ones that . . .

Here, Miss Matterhorn suddenly appeared at Dexter's elbow, dropped a large muscular hand on the note that he was writing and swept it up in front of her nose.

"This-could-be-one-of-the-strange-ones-that," read Miss Matterhorn out loud to the class. She peered down at Dexter.

"What strange ones?" she asked with an air of innocence. "To what *strange ones* does this note refer?"

Dexter turned a shade paler than usual. "To no ones," he answered weakly. "I mean, to no one. It doesn't refer to people."

"Not to people, no. But to teachers?" Miss Matterhorn's eyes flashed. "You see, I have caught your meaning, Mr. Drake, crafty as you have tried to be. Teachers are not people, are they? They are members of a subhuman animal species that gathers in herds on the school grounds every morning at eight o'clock. Is that correct?"

"Oh, no," whimpered Dexter, for he could see that Miss Matterhorn was going into one of her famous wild fits.

"From there, they gallop to the teachers' lounge, bury their snouts in troughs of coffee and crow insanely at each other," Miss Matterhorn went on, mixing her animals up so badly that the picture in Dexter's mind was of some horrible intergalactic creature.

Miss Matterhorn tapped her pencil three times on Dexter's desk while the whole class swallowed hard.

"And then!" she cried. "And then, the herd separates and trots off, each to its appointed stall—or classroom, so called—where it spends the day bleating and bahing and making a fuss. Am I right, Mr. Drake? Are these the sort of *strange ones* you had in mind?"

Miss Matterhorn seemed now to have settled on goats. Actually, she did look a little like a drawing of the biggest Billy Goat Gruff which Dexter remembered from a book in his childhood. He glanced up at her anxiously and then over at his friend. Howlie had slumped far down under his desk and was obviously in no position to send aid.

"Mr. Drake, you are in disgrace!"

"But Miss Matterhorn . . ."

"You will now go to the hall and stand there for ten minutes while you think over the nature of your disgrace."

"But Miss Matterhorn . . ."

"And you will think also about the true nature of teachers, who are human after all. . . ." Miss Matterhorn took a tissue from the sleeve of her sweater. "Very human, indeed, and have feelings which are easily hurt," she concluded in a quivery voice.

She walked back to her desk while Dexter went red-faced to the hall. Meanwhile, the class examined its fingernails.

Everyone was rather shocked by Miss Matterhorn's confession about being human. It took something away from her that no one had expected ever to be taken away. Certain braver students looked cautiously over their shoulders toward the back of the room. They were afraid Miss Matterhorn might be weeping.

Luckily, she had put her tissue back up her sleeve and seemed to have control of herself.

Of course, there was no question in anyone's mind after this that Miss Matterhorn really was one of the "strange ones." Dexter's note had described her perfectly, even if it had been about something else. In fact, Miss M. was not only strange but positively unhealthy and she should be taken to a hospital as soon as possible before it was too late. Everyone said so.

Everyone, that is, but Dexter. He did not say these things or hear them said. He was brooding, as if on some great disaster. Gone were his swagger and his theatrical air. The incident with Miss Matterhorn throbbed in his head, not only that day but on through the night. And when, the following morning, Howlie took him off to a corner of the schoolyard to talk, he saw his friend slink across the dirt like a beaten dog. Dexter looked exhausted. He seemed on the verge of tears.

"This is terrible. Terrible," he muttered. "To be caught passing notes by a blind woman. And then to get sent to the hall!" He glanced at Howlie in agony. "I almost died out there, do you know that? Whenever anyone walked by, I almost died."

"Don't take it so hard," said Howlie. "It happens to everyone at least once. It doesn't mean anything."

"Yes it does. It means something," Dexter said. "It means I've sunk lower than ever. I'm not only a mouse, I'm a stupid mouse. And every person in this school knows it."

"No they don't," Howlie said. "They aren't talking about you. Miss Matterhorn's the one they're talking about."

Dexter paid no attention. He was caught up in his own view of things.

"I've been thinking of what to do," he told Howlie. "Our

plan for getting Bulldog Calhoun looks pretty dumb all of a sudden."

"Dumb!" exclaimed Howlie. "But I've got everything ready—the blood, the knives. Besides, I talked to Bulldog after school yesterday. He said he might come. He said: See you on Saturday you little creep. It sounded as if he'd be there."

"Well, tell him to forget it," Dexter said. "We aren't doing that plan anymore."

"What?"

"I've decided not to do it. I've got a better idea."

"You've decided!" said Howlie. "What about me? Dexter, what's wrong with you?"

"Listen, we've got to improve our image, right? So relax and let me handle this," Dexter said in a queer, tight voice. "I'm the idea man around here and the idea I have is this: We'll go for the diamonds. We'll con the farmer into letting us dig under the tree. We might even be able to squeeze him for some clues to where the chest is hidden."

"Squeeze him!" cried Howlie. "Come on. The farmer isn't somebody you should squeeze."

"Because diamonds are big business," Dexter went on. "When we find them, everybody in town will be impressed, not just Bulldog Calhoun. Also, we'll be rich."

"Wait a minute. The farmer will be rich, not us. If the diamonds are there, they're on his land."

"Howlie, don't be such a wimp. Think what Bulldog would do if he found the treasure. He'd keep some of the diamonds for himself, right? The farmer would never know."

"But that's stealing!"

"So what?"

Howlie stared at his friend. Dexter had played a lot of parts over the years, but he'd never acted like this before. "Are you feeling okay?" Howlie asked him. "I don't get it. Why are you being such a rat all of a sudden?"

Dexter narrowed his eyes in a way that made him appear even more rat-like.

"Because I am one," he said. "It's about time, too. And now that I think about it, I don't need you along on this. So I guess we might as well split up."

"I guess so," Howlie said angrily.

"And don't tell anyone what I'm doing," Dexter said.

"You think I'd tell?"

"And don't come around asking me for a share in the treasure after I've found it."

"Dexter! What happened to you out in the hall? You've gone crazy."

Dexter turned his back and walked away
across the playground.

THE SWAMI appeared calm and reasonable as he ordered new clothes for his troops. He was neither. Beneath his cool facade he was a boiling cauldron. Close observers might have noticed the beads of sweat steaming on his forehead, the rattling of his bony hands. While his loyal followers galloped into the shop's fitting room and harassed the salesman for correct sizes, the swami edged out a back door to stand on his head in an alley. Despite the swami's great intelligence, he was a human being like any other and not always in control of himself.

The truth was, the swami was obsessed by the magnificent oak tree. He could think of nothing else. Like a fiery beacon on a black night it drew him. Or rather, it gripped his imagination like a large, leafy hand and dragged it, twitching, across oceans and continents.

The swami was not pleased to find himself in the position of being dragged. He had believed himself above and beyond such things. What a mistake! Before the oak he had become as helpless as a child in the grip of a powerful mother.

"Non-stop. Non-stop. We must fly non-stop," his followers heard him murmuring under his breath. Some mistook his words for a new prayer or mantra, and began to mumble along with him.

"Non-stop. Non-stop. We must fly non-stop," hummed the swami's troops as they followed their leader on board the airplane at Bombay airport. The followers settled their small, wiry bodies in the plane's seats and tried to sit still. A stewardess came by to help them with their seat belts.

"Stop wiggling!" she ordered. "How can I connect your belts when you are slithering around and humming that way."

As it turned out, the flight was not non-stop. The airplane was forced to land in Paris to correct a small malfunction. It was nothing to worry about, the passengers were informed: only a few hours' wait at most. Anyone who wished to disembark should do so quickly.

Paris? Memories rustled in the swami's head. How many years had passed since he had last been in that city? He recalled a rainy spring during his student days. Or was it a rainy autumn? He remembered a stroll along the banks of the Seine with a certain person. Fi Fi was her name. Or was that a French poodle he'd known? The swami sighed. The past is such a slippery animal. One can never quite get one's hands around it.

Of course, the swami had no intention of visiting Paris again. He was fixed on his tree. Besides, there were the goats and peacocks to consider. The loyal followers had insisted on bringing every last one of them. They had been packed into the plane's pressurized baggage compartment and could not be easily moved.

Nevertheless, Paris! There is a certain charm, a certain

air about it, no? Glamorous shops, glittering women, perfume adrift on the Champs-Élysées, enfin. Who can resist such a tempting place?

Suddenly, the swami could not. He rose from his seat and herded his followers, now dressed to the teeth in high Indian fashion, off the plane, through the airline terminal, toward "les taxis."

"Just a quick trip to town," he assured his followers. "You must see the Eiffel Tower. Can't we leave those goats behind? Just a fast trot through the Arch of Triumph. It has been years since I was last in Paris! Must we have those peacocks bunching and scratching up the floor?"

The swami did not expect to spend more than an hour or two in Paris. He expected to be back in his seat aboard the airplane, sipping Indian tea, long before take-off.

However, the Arch of Triumph proved to be an enormous success among the followers. Looking up at it, their eyes bulged slightly, then flattened with wonder and fear. The arch seemed as big as a mountain to them, and was carved all over with terrible scenes of war and death.

"Napoleon," the followers whispered among themselves. "Who is this great swami Napoleon, builder of such a mountain?"

They ran their eyes hungrily over the names, carved in stone, of the battles he had won. They knelt at the tomb of the unknown soldier. They wandered under the arch in twos and threes, feeling deliciously small and insignificant. The swami could not drag them away. He seemed to have lost his power to control them.

"We want Napoleon! We want Napoleon!" the followers chanted in quiet but insistent voices.

"But he has been dead for over one hundred and fifty years!" cried the swami. "It is only his arch that remains. Come. We must leave now if we are to make our plane."

Dead! And for so long! The followers were crestfallen. They peered around corners of the arch, as if they expected the great general to appear anyway. They wept together in small, damp knots of arms. It is not often one comes across a leader of such immense power and charm as Napoleon the First of France. Oh, to be the follower of such a leader! By comparison, the swami—well, ahem. The followers glanced at him over their shoulders and remarked to each other how the long trip had certainly worn him down. He seemed smaller, suddenly, and grayer, and—dare they mention it?—he had been acting oddly over an oak tree in recent days. Should they call in a doctor to examine him?

"Oh, Napoleon. Give us a sign," prayed the loyal followers.

At last, only the promise of ice cream and pastries persuaded them to leave the arch. They allowed themselves to be taken to a sidewalk café where they ordered glacé chocolate and eclairs and large cups of ice water. These they shared, when the waiter wasn't looking, with the goats and peacocks, whom they kept hidden beneath the starched white cloths on the tables.

By now, it was nearing sundown and the swami, hearing the church bells of Paris begin to chime, realized that they had missed their plane. Ah, well. It happens to the best of us. "C'est la vie," the swami mused philosophically.

"And," he added under his breath, "what a relief to be rid of that tyrant oak tree."

There is no doubt that he had already drifted under the spell of Paris. Even as he watched, the gay lights of the city began to come on up and down the Champs-Élysées. The flying buttresses of Notre Dame were illuminated.

The swami leaned back carelessly in his chair at the café. Though he was not a smoker, he lit the end of a thin cigar and blew a series of elegant smoke rings. He bought a newspaper, though his French was poor, and tried to read the headlines. He ogled passing women. He ordered wine. And more wine.

The swami was enjoying himself more than he had in years, toasting the health of French poodles and cracking jokes. Soon he had his followers in stitches of laughter. Helplessly, they rolled on the floor under the starched white table cloths, where they became entangled with the goats and peacocks.

Feathers clogged the air. Fleece flew. The followers could not stop laughing, especially after the swami did an ingenious imitation of the airline stewardess who had attended them on their flight from Bombay. Ha, ha, ha! Admittedly, her skirt had been a trifle tight. Hee, hee, hee!

"Pardon, Monsieur."

Oh, dear. It was the manager of the café.

"Monsieur, je regret . . ."

Oh my. They had made quite a mess, they saw, when they looked about. How had all those wine glasses smashed on the floor?

The followers stumbled to their feet. They were escorted to the sidewalk while the swami was forced to settle the bill, which seemed ridiculously high. The manager was speaking French like a machine gun. The waiter was yelling and pointing under the tables where the goats had left an unsightly sprinkling of pellets. The swami's face burned with embarrassment. How could he have made such a fool of himself?

"We must find a good hotel for the night," he told his loyal followers crossly when he joined them on the sidewalk. "No more trouble."

Everyone was cross by this time, and they were all blaming each other for what had happened.

"Your manners are deplorable," the swami told his followers. "I was appalled. One would think you had been brought up in the depths of a cave."

"It wasn't us," the followers cried. "It was the goats.

They would not stay underneath the tables and kept tripping us up."

The goats, meanwhile, blamed the peacocks, whose feathers tickled unbearably at close quarters, while the peacocks blamed the goats for their sharp hooves.

"Onward!" roared the angry swami over the hubbub. "Stop squawking. Keep walking. We will go to the Ritz. They always have plenty of room."

All morning, the farmer sat alone on his living room couch with his legs propped up on the coffee table. It was Friday, the day before his eightieth birthday. He was listening to the wind whistle around his house. There was a harsh sound in it, a cold rattle, a dry chatter, that the farmer recognized. October was nearly over. Winter was coming. The farmer pulled his old sweater more closely to him and tried to remember younger birthdays in his life. Had the weather always been so depressing?

Early in the afternoon, someone knocked on his door.

"Come in!" called the farmer without getting up. He took his legs off the coffee table, moving each leg with his hands as if it were an object not connected to him. Then he looked up and squinted toward the door.

The visitor appeared to be a stranger. He was a small-sized boy wearing a wrinkled windbreaker and a crafty expression on his face. Who in blazes could it be? The farmer leaned forward and squinted harder.

"Dexter Drake!" he exclaimed at last. "I must be going blind. For a minute I couldn't tell who you were. Glad to see you! Come and sit down. Bad wind we're having. What's on your mind?"

"I haven't seen you out lately. I wondered if you were sick," Dexter said, sliding into a chair. "We get out of school early on Fridays," he added, then folded his hands and looked at the farmer in a most calculating way, as if he were counting the hairs on his head.

"Nothing much wrong with me," the farmer replied with a shrug. "There's nobody much out there so why should I go out?"

"There's me," said Dexter.

"So there is!" The farmer beamed with pleasure. "You and your friend, Howlie. I've been watching you both out under my tree. You're up to something, aren't you? I was just saying the other day: Those boys are up to something."

The farmer was about to give Dexter a wink to let him know that he had been a boy once himself and knew what it was to be up to things. Just then he saw Dexter's face take on a mean, secretive look that was more unpleasant than ever. "Watch out," the look said. "Don't tell the old idiot anything."

The farmer sat back on the couch and gazed out the window.

"Winter's coming," he remarked, coldly. "Seems like it's getting here quicker this year."

"We weren't doing anything under the tree," Dexter said in his new, sly voice. "You don't have to worry about us. Anyway, Howlie and I aren't friends anymore."

"That so?" The farmer glanced up.

"He's a creep," Dexter said.

"A what?"

"We split up," Dexter said, louder, so the poor old farmer would understand. "We had a fight and . . ."

 "You needn't shout," snapped the farmer, cutting him

off. "I can hear you perfectly well." He looked out the window again and a silence settled over the room. Dexter glanced around nervously. He cleared his throat and spoke again:

"You sure have a good view of the oak tree from here. And by the way, has anybody ever looked for the pirate's treasure chest that's supposedly buried out there? Was it ever found, I mean? I was just wondering," said Dexter, in a voice that sounded false even to his own ears.

For a moment it appeared that the farmer might not have heard the question. He sat motionless on the couch. Then, slowly, he brought his eyes in from outside the window. He rested them on Dexter's face.

"Diamonds," he said. "So that's what you're after."

"Oh, no," protested Dexter. "I'm just doing some research on old stories."

The farmer smiled. He shifted to a new position on the couch and rubbed his knees.

"People have looked for that chest," he said. "In fact, they've spent a good amount of their time looking for it. But so far, they haven't found it."

"They haven't?" said Dexter.

"This was a while back," the farmer said, still rubbing. "Probably about seventy years ago."

"Does that mean the story is true?" Dexter asked.

Maybe the farmer really had grown deaf in the last few months. He didn't seem to hear this question either.

"I'll tell you a secret," he said suddenly. He leaned

toward Dexter, who thought for a moment that he was going to reveal a clue to the treasure's hiding place. But his subject was quite different.

"Something's happened to my memory," the old farmer whispered, with glowing eyes. "It's getting sharper by the day. I can't understand it, but I've been remembering everything lately, things that happened way back when I was a boy no bigger than you. I was just now remembering how I went digging for those diamonds myself. My friends laughed at me, told me I was crazy. But I went right ahead. Nobody could tell me anything back in those days."

Dexter stared at him in surprise. "You went digging for the treasure?" he said.

"It's strange, I know," the farmer continued brightly. "An old fellow like me. You'd expect the opposite. You'd expect me to be losing my mind instead of sharpening it up. Sometimes I sit a whole afternoon on this couch remembering one thing after another. It's a good way to travel for a man with bad knees." The farmer chuckled. "A fine way to travel.

"There's something I'm worried about, though," he went on, fixing Dexter with his eye to make sure of his attention. "Who's going to do the remembering around here after I'm gone. What do you think about that?"

"I don't know," said Dexter.

 "Exactly," replied the farmer. A queer look flashed over

his face. "I don't know either. It's a question, all right. A big question."

The farmer coughed—ahunk!—and spoke again.

"I don't mind you digging if that's what you want to do," he told Dexter. "There are shovels in the barn."

"There are?"

"Don't dig up the oak's roots, though," he warned. "And don't smash through them. That tree's special to me and I don't intend any harm to come to it. You can get on pretty well by digging in between, if I remember right."

"Are you sure? Are you sure it's all right?" Dexter had his regular voice back again.

"I think I used a pickax one time with good results," the farmer said. "There's one in the barn hanging up on the wall."

"Yes, sir!"

"Hold on a minute. There's another thing." The farmer waved Dexter away from the door.

"It's the rule around here and always has been that anybody who finds anything lying on the ground or in the ground, well, it's the finder's property. The owner of the land has no right to it."

The farmer announced this exciting piece of information with his eyes looking outside the window again. "But I'd be happy if you'd let me know how the work progresses from time to time," he added.

"Oh yes. I will."

"And you might come by tomorrow, it's Saturday, and give me a report then," the farmer said without glancing around. "If it's convenient, that is. If not, don't bother."

"Oh, it will be convenient," Dexter assured him, with a sudden feeling of warmth toward the old man. "I'll come tomorrow, for sure. And thank you," he added in a lower, embarrassed tone that sounded more like an apology.

"No need for thanks," answered the farmer. "I know what buried treasure can do to a fellow." He pointed at the door. "Go on. Get started. I need a rest."

"Yes, sir!" cried Dexter, racing away. He couldn't wait to get his hands on a shovel.

4

M*y dear friends. As I stand here beneath our great oak on this golden October day, I am reminded of happy days gone by which . . .*

Mrs. Trawley stopped writing and nibbled the end of her pen. It was Friday, the day before the big rally, and she was seated in a pool of afternoon sunlight on her glassed-in porch trying to write her speech. She had written "golden" because, at the moment, the day was golden. But suppose tomorrow were rainy? It would be difficult to change the speech, she discovered:

My dear friends. As I stand here beneath our great oak on this chilly, wet and altogether gloomy October day . . .

No. No. It would never do. Mrs. Trawley tore the page off

her pad and began a new speech that was not dependent on the weather.

My dear friends. I stand before you today to speak simply and openly on behalf of our Dimpole Oak. For though time like an ever rolling stream bears all its sons away, this oak remains, as it has remained and will remain for many years to come. I hope, barring the unforeseen, life being at the mercy of variable winds, as a symbol of . . .

Mrs. Trawley stopped writing again and nibbled. The pen was not big enough to really bite into, she noticed with a frown. She took a stick of gum out of her pocket, unwrapped it and slipped it into her mouth.

But even chewing did not help this second beginning of the speech. Somehow it had gone astray. Far from coming out simply and openly in a long silken string of words like the Gettysburg Address, it had bumped and twisted and rolled itself up into a terrible knot.

"I must not let my sentences run away from me like this," Mrs. Trawley told herself severely. "I must organize and control them. I am not sure either," she muttered, "that 'My dear friends' is a good opening. After all, many of these people are not my dear friends and some of them are not my friends at all."

Mrs. Trawley unwrapped another stick of gum and added it to the first in her mouth. She could not help thinking, now that she was on the subject of people, how very difficult they could be. Her experience of organizing the oak tree rally during the past week was a perfect example.

Everyone in Dimpole had agreed that the oak tree was in danger. Everyone had voted to do something about it. And then no one had ventured a single idea. It was interesting to see how people hung back timidly and waited to be served with a plan. But when Mrs. Trawley had presented them with the very plan they needed, when she had told them clearly what ought to be done, they had coughed and scratched and brought up niggling objections.

Further, when asked to volunteer for jobs, they had hidden, or they had gone out on their own and bungled the work, or they had fought among themselves and accomplished nothing.

Trying to organize people was like trying to herd goats, Mrs. Trawley decided, as she sat on her back porch squinting into the sun. It was a matter of staying constantly on patrol, nipping a hind foot here, heading a stray off there, until the whole bleating mass of animals was maneuvered down the mountain and into the barn. Mrs. Trawley sighed. Perhaps it was better not to bother with organizing, she thought, but just to go ahead and do everything oneself like Henny Penny. She picked up her pen and began to write again.

Ladies and Gentlemen: Let me assure you that I do not

intend to bore you today with flowery language or extended metaphors on the nature of things. Let me go right to the point and say that the reason I have organized this excellent rally, the reason you are all here listening to me attentively, the reason I am standing up here giving this great speech is that the great Dimpole Oak is in danger. Yes, danger, I repeat.

When she had finished writing this opening, Mrs. Trawley sat back and smiled triumphantly. At last she was on the right track. It is wonderful how a good speech just naturally develops a rhythm of its own, she thought, blowing a small bubble to celebrate.

The gum had turned out to be a stringy kind of bubble gum. Most likely a cheap brand, always a mistake to buy. She unwrapped another piece and combined it with the wad in her mouth. Oh, yes. Much better. Her second bubble was quite a good size one.

"Now, where were we?" murmured Mrs. Trawley, looking down at her speech again. "It is so very pleasant to be in control of things," she added, chewing vigorously on the gum.

The telephone rang. Mrs. Trawley rose from her chair and went inside the house to answer it.

"Hello (chomp, chomp)?"

There was a moment of silence, and then the sound of someone breathing heavily on the other end of the line.

"Hello? Hello?"

She heard the click of a receiver being carefully hung up.

"How annoying," Mrs. Trawley said. "Who can it have been?" She glanced around the living room and then went to a front window to look outside. A stiff wind was blowing the bushes about. The day was not nearly as warm as it had seemed on the glassed-in porch, she realized.

"I am sure it was someone calling about the rally," Mrs. Trawley told herself. "They were probably interrupted and will call again in a minute."

She waited, with growing anxiety, by the window. No one called back.

"How silly," murmured Mrs. Trawley. She began to chew faster and to imagine terrible things.

The caller was a burglar testing to see if she was home.

The caller was a murderer testing to see if she was home alone.

The caller was an escaped convict looking for a place to hide for the night.

"Oh, dear! Oh, dear!" Suddenly, Mrs. Trawley was terrified, although she knew it was absurd. The golden afternoon had taken on an evil shine.

"I will take my speech to the public library and finish it there," she said, trying to control her wild feelings. "And I will call Mr. Trawley at his office and arrange to have dinner with him at a restaurant. I know I am being a complete coward, but . . ."

Mrs. Trawley gathered up her pad, pens, purse, coat
and another package of bubblegum and fled out
the front door. A minute later, she
was in her large, black car
speeding down the
road toward
Dimpole.

DURING ALL THE TIME that Mrs. Trawley sat on her porch writing her speech (before the frightening phone call drove her away), Miss Shirley Hand was at her own home, across town. She was not sitting comfortably in a pool of sunlight, though. The young teacher was in trouble. From one end of her small apartment to the other she walked, patting her forehead with lime-green tissues.

There was a whole box of tissues on the dining room table, along with a bottle of lavender-scented cologne. Whenever she passed the table, Miss Hand drew a tissue from the box and doused it with cologne. Then she dabbed at her face and went off pacing again. The apartment reeked of lavender. The cat had taken refuge under the bed.

"Oh, why do I get myself into these horrid corners?" Miss Hand moaned to herself. "Why didn't I think of a Special Entertainment for Great Dimpole Oak Day long ago? I put it off and put it off until time ran out. The rally is tomorrow! Now, there is nothing to do but call Mrs. Trawley and tell her I have failed. Failed!" wailed Miss Hand. "Oh, I do hate failing more than anything else."

She sat on the living room couch beside the telephone and eyed it fearfully.

Failing Mrs. Trawley was bad enough, she thought. What was worse was to be failing right out in plain view of everyone in Dimpole. For Mrs. Trawley had been telling people about Miss Hand's Special Entertainment. She had been whetting their appetites with enticing remarks, and even boasting about "Shirley's Big Secret."

"What on earth is going to happen? What wonderful thing do you have planned for us?" Miss Matterhorn had asked Miss Hand at school only yesterday. And when Miss Hand had protested, "It's really nothing! I wouldn't expect anything," Miss Matterhorn had given her a sly look and said:

"Shirley Hand, you are far too humble for your own good. You never give yourself enough credit."

Too humble? Oh, dear! Miss Hand sprang up from the couch when she recalled Miss Matterhorn's well-meaning words. She strode across to the dining room table where she snatched up a mass of lime tissues and drowned them in cologne. Miss Hand disliked disappointing well-meaning people even more than she minded failing.

"Loopy, I must take action," she said to the cat, who had chosen this moment to tiptoe bravely through the fumes in search of his litter box.

"I must sit down and call Mrs. Trawley this minute! I will tell her," she added, picking up the telephone receiver, "that I have not arranged a Special Entertainment due to unforeseen circumstances, and that she must announce it at the rally tomorrow so that people do not expect anything."

 Unforeseen circumstances? Miss Hand couldn't help

giggling under the tissues she was holding to her face. It sounded so mysterious, as if she had entered the pages of one of her mystery stories.

Miss Hand dialed Mrs. Trawley's number.

The phone rang several times. Miss Hand remembered that Mrs. Trawley liked to sit on her porch on pleasant afternoons. Or was she out altogether?

Finally, Mrs. Trawley answered: "Hello?"

Miss Hand froze. The sound of Mrs. Trawley's voice undid her completely. She could not utter a word, could not even begin to talk about "unforeseen circumstances." Her heart beat wildly. Her breath came in short gasps.

After what seemed to be a long time, Miss Hand lowered the receiver and hung up. She stared at the floor. Mrs. Trawley had been chewing something, she recalled vaguely. What could she have been eating at four o'clock in the afternoon?

"Oh, dear. What shall I do?" cried Miss Hand in a muffled voice of agony. By now she had such a large mound of tissues pressed to her face that anyone catching sight of her would have thought she had a toothache.

Miss Hand was plunged into a deep pit of despair by her phone call to Mrs. Trawley. How could she have acted so cowardly? she asked herself. She was a worm, a mouse, a sparrow of a person. Not only had she failed to organize a Special Entertainment for Great Dimpole Oak Day, but she had failed to tell Mrs. Trawley that she had failed.

There was no excuse for what she had done. None at all. When people act like worms and mice what can anyone do except . . . except . . .

Miss Hand sat motionless on her living room couch absorbed in these dreadful thoughts. Even when her own telephone began to ring, she did not at first hear it. And finally, when she did hear—oh horrors! She looked around the room with new fear in her eyes. Could the caller be Mrs. Trawley checking to see that the Special Entertainment was in order? Oh, yes! She was sure it was Mrs. Trawley. She positively knew it.

"H-h-h-hello?" said Miss Hand cringingly into the receiver.

"Shirley, this is me, Mrs. Trawley. I'm calling to make sure your Special Entertainment for the rally tomorrow is in order. Perhaps we could meet this evening so that you can go over the details with me?"

STRANGE as it may seem, these words were imaginary. No one ever said them. Miss Hand believed she heard Mrs. Trawley saying them, but she was mistaken. Her frantic mind had jumped its track. She heard what she expected to hear or, perhaps, what she thought she deserved to hear. The caller was not Mrs. Trawley. It was Mr. Glover. This is what was really said:

"Shirley? It's me, Harvey. I'm calling to make sure you

can march with me to the rally tomorrow. But, perhaps we could meet this evening also? Would you care to go for a walk in the country with me?"

"SHIRLEY? Shirley! It's Harvey Glover. I am not Mrs. Trawley!" Mr. Glover shouted into the telephone. "Shirley? Are you all right? I am not calling about Special Entertainments. Stop raving and pull yourself together."

Several minutes passed before Miss Hand could do this. Afterwards, she was delighted to accept Mr. Glover's invitation to walk. Would he mind having the cat along, too? she asked. It badly needed to get out of the house.

MEANWHILE, in a hayfield just outside of town, the figure of a boy digging furiously under a tree was visible to motorists passing in the road.

What was the kid up to? several drivers asked themselves. Was he looking for arrowheads? Burying his dead dog? Making a swimming hole? There were any number of possibilities.

Unaware that he was being examined, Dexter Drake spit on the palms of his hands and frowned. He knew the pirates' diamonds were close by. They lay just beneath the earth at the bottom of the Dimpole Oak, between its big, plunging roots. Some people, it is said, have an extra sense. They don't have to hear or see or smell a thing to know it is there. Dexter thought he must have an extra sense, not in all cases but in the special case of this treasure. The diamonds were sending him messages:

"Dig here, immediately!"

"Over here is where we are!"

"Look at me! Look at me," they called in voices that would have sounded bright and sharp if they had been audible through the normal human sense of hearing. Dexter heard them with his extra sense—he couldn't have explained how—and he attacked the ground fiercely. Though the day was cool and blowy, he began to sweat, partly because the digging was hard work, partly from excitement. He expected with every shovelful of dirt to see the treasure appear.

Perhaps the diamonds were upset by their approaching rescue. They were sending out garbled messages, it seemed. Dexter dug here and there about the tree, always careful to avoid its tender roots as the farmer had requested. But he found nothing during the first hour.

Was he digging deep enough? he wondered. He took off his jacket and set about widening and deepening the holes. Still, as the afternoon wore on, he turned up only an old-fashioned jackknife, rusted shut. It was far too small to have been responsible for any of the oak tree murders, Dexter saw with disappointment. There was a word or a few letters etched into the metal on one side. He couldn't make them out under the grime.

Howlie would be interested in this knife, Dexter thought. He would know how to soak it and clean it with special fluids. He could probably make it work again. Dexter turned his head and looked down the long field where the oak grew. He looked across the next field and the next to a distant clump of trees which he knew to be the shade trees protecting Howlie's house. Nothing was moving there.

After a while, Dexter began to dig again. The farmer came out and hobbled downhill to watch.

"Good work. Keep it up," he said, peering cheerfully at the excavation. But he didn't look well and left soon after.

By sunset, Dexter was tired and growing impatient. The area around the oak tree was pockmarked with holes, and large, untidy piles of dirt lay everywhere. Besides this, the voices of the diamonds had become thin and pale as whispers. Dexter's extra sense could not always tell from which direction they came. It was not the fault of his extra sense.

"The diamonds are playing with me," he murmured.

He began to suspect them of trickery, of calling out to him like frightened children and then hiding mischievously when he came to find them. In the most maddening way, the diamonds seemed to move right out from under his shovel. He was always left a little behind, running from one hole to the next, with an idea that the diamonds were there just ahead of him, just ahead.

Then evening fell and the voices of the diamonds disappeared altogether. A wind blew through the branches of the Dimpole Oak. It caused the remaining leaves to flutter mournfully. A few leaves chose this dark moment to drop off. They swirled down and surprised Dexter. He had never thought about leaves dropping off trees at night. And yet, they must do it all the time, he knew. Leaves must fall in the dark every night, sailing down to the black ground by themselves, with no one to see them go.

Dexter shivered. He began to feel abandoned. He continued to dig for a while, but he knew the diamonds had gone away. He would never find them now.

Oh, those diamonds! When Dexter thought about them he grew hot. His chest ached. He wanted to dig them up. He wished to hold them in his hands.

 Suddenly, with the same ache, Dexter wanted Howlie.

He missed him terribly. Howlie always made him feel so pleased with himself. He cheered him up in gloomy times and toned him down when his ideas got too wild. And he was reliable. He was always there, keeping Dexter going.

Not anymore. Dexter had driven him away.

"I've been acting like a creep. What will I do now?" Dexter said, muttering to himself, as he looked off into the darkness.

He was becoming a little frightened. Why had he stayed so late? The wind was coming up and the oak tree was making eerie noises. It moaned and whined in a way that Dexter had never heard before. It flailed its branches and twisted itself around like an enormous octopus, as if it were angry at Dexter for some reason. And, in between the gusts of wind . . . what was that? Dexter thought he heard voices. Not diamond voices, human ones.

"Who is it? Who's there?" Dexter shouted into the dark. The angry tree was thrashing overhead.

"I can hear you!" cried Dexter. "Who are you? What do you want?"

There was no answer: only a great creak came from the oak's trunk. Then out of the blackness two long shapes rose up.

Dexter stood still, frozen with terror.

BUT WHEN the shapes approached, they turned out to be nothing more than Miss Hand from the Dimpole School second grade and Mr. Glover from the post office. Dexter knew them both and they knew him.

"Oh!" gasped Miss Hand. "It's only Dexter Drake. Thank goodness!" She was holding on tightly to Mr. Glover. Her face appeared pale in the darkness.

"We thought you were a ghost," she said, laughing.

"We thought you were a murderer disposing of the body," Mr. Glover chimed in. He put his arm around Miss Hand, then looked at it with a frown, as if it had gotten away from him and done something unexpected.

"We thought all sorts of things," said Miss Hand, snuggling against the arm, "but what we really thought was that you were the farmer."

"The farmer!" Dexter said in surprise. Now that he was over his first fright, the scene seemed unreal to him: the unlikely pair erupting out of the dark, the wind whipping the tree overhead, the talk of ghosts and murderers. He felt as if he had come into the middle of one of the farmer's stories.

"We thought," said Miss Hand, moving closer to Dexter and lowering her voice secretively, "we thought you were the evil farmer up to no good. We heard the shovel scraping in the dirt and we were afraid he would rush out and grab us."

"And bury us alive!" giggled Mr. Glover. He was acting a little strangely, leaning first forward, then backwards, as if he were thinking of kissing Miss Hand but at the last moment changed his mind.

"Which farmer?" Dexter asked in amazement. "Do you mean that farmer?" He pointed up the hill to the farmer's house. "But . . . he's not evil at all. He would never jump out and grab anyone. Even if he could jump," Dexter added, "which he can't anymore because of his knees."

"His knees?" Miss Hand murmured. She was gazing into Mr. Glover's eyes and he was gazing back at her with the same surprised frown on his face as when his arm had escaped. Neither of them paid any more attention to Dexter, and his words about the farmer passed over their heads.

"Oh, Harvey, what a romantic place," sighed Miss Hand. She stepped up to the windblown oak and leaned lazily against its trunk, as if she were leaning back on the feather cushions of a great sofa.

"Oh, Shirley," said Mr. Glover, following her to the tree and stepping in several of Dexter's holes. "I knew you would like it here."

He leaned against the tree beside her. They both gazed heavenward through the thrashing branches, as if they expected to see stars up there. Actually, a storm had arrived. The wind had blown layers of clouds into the area. Drops of rain were already splashing down. Dexter put on his jacket and turned up the collar. He looked around for the pickax.

"I could stay here forever," Mr. Glover was telling Miss Hand, as the wind shrieked and tore at his clothes. "This has always been my favorite place. Ever since I was a boy.

I used to come here to ride on that big root over there. I'd make up the most exciting stories about masked bandits and the pony express."

"You must tell me one," said Miss Hand, while from overhead came the sound of wood splintering and a good-sized branch was hurled by the wind at their feet.

Dexter found the pickax, grabbed the shovel and fled. He ran uphill to the barn where he stowed the tools, then he ran downhill past the tree. The fallen branch had made no impression on Miss Hand and Mr. Glover. They were off in another world whispering to each other and holding hands. Their hair whipped about their faces.

"Watch out! Be careful!" Dexter tried to shout as he went by, but the rain had begun to fall harder and his voice was drowned out. He put his head down and raced blindly across the fields. He was going to Howlie's house. He was going even though it was late and stormy, though he was wet and dirty. He had to see Howlie immediately.

"I don't know what got into me," Dexter practiced saying to Howlie as he ran with the rain streaming down his face. "You were right and I was wrong."

Was it too late now to go back to the first plan? Dexter wondered. Howlie probably hated him by now. Overhead, lightning flashed. A terrifying roll of thunder echoed from one end of the valley to the other.

"I went sort of crazy over the diamonds," Dexter went on, practicing between pants. "I must've dug a hundred holes. I thought the diamonds were talking to me. Then Miss Hand came out of nowhere with Mr. Glover from the post office. I could swear I saw a black cat, too."

It sounded crazy, all right. What would Howlie say?

Dexter ran faster. He felt as if something were chasing him, something big and wild and leafy like the oak tree. But when he looked over his shoulder, nothing was there. He turned and ran on through the dark.

In Paris, it was four o'clock in the morning. (Seven hours always separate Paris and Dimpole on the clock, with Paris coming in front.)

From his fancy bedroom at the Ritz Hotel, the swami was trying to tune in to the Dimpole Oak. He had been trying for several hours with no success. There was some sort of interference on the line, apparently at the oak tree end. The swami suspected this because whichever way he routed his meditations—up through South America, down through Canada, across the Bermuda Triangle and so on, at a certain point he would run into the same wildly thrashing currents. They were such powerful currents that if the swami had not known better, he would have thought the tree in the midst of a violent storm.

But the swami did know better.

"This is all my fault," he moaned, as he slumped on his canopied bed. "I have angered the tree. It's no use blaming my loyal followers, much as I would like to. I am the one who has done it. Such silly behavior. Such poor self-control."

The swami buried his face in a pillow when he recalled the scene in the café earlier that evening.

"Now the oak has cut communications and left me to stew in my own soup," the swami went on bitterly. "I can't get through to it. It won't receive me. But perhaps if I navigated up the Mississippi River and came eastward across the Great Lakes begging for forgiveness? I will give it one more shot."

It was no use. The swami's inner eye was foiled again. Red flashes and electric zig-zags filled its screen. All sounds, smells and views of the holy tree were eclipsed.

"Let this be a lesson to us all," the distraught swami could not help calling out to his troops. "From now on, we will always travel non-stop."

"Non-stop," droned the sleepy followers, who lay in limp heaps about the room. They had never been so tired in their lives. The evening at the café had worn them out. They hoped and prayed that the swami would go to sleep soon. Really, he was becoming impossible, they whispered among themselves, first dragging them halfway around the world on the pretext of visiting a tree, then changing his mind and leaping into the thick of Paris, then plying them with wine, then keeping them up all night worrying about himself. Napoleon would never have acted so irrationally.

"Oh, Napoleon. Give us a sign," the followers prayed. "We know you are there. Don't fool around with us anymore."

The swami, however, was not about to go to sleep. How could he sleep at a time like this? The more he thought about the oak the more frantic he became. He was drowning and help was out of reach. He was falling with no one below to catch him.

"Holy Master, you must not work yourself into such a lather," the yawning followers counseled. "Lie down and rest. You will feel better in the morning."

"Rest?" the swami repeated in amazement. "Rest indeed!" he cried. "We have no time to rest. We must leave for America at once."

"Leave!" shrieked the followers.

"Immediately. There is not a moment to lose if we are going to save ourselves. Get up. Up!" shouted the swami, poking the followers with his toes. "We will have to fly stand-by and we will probably be separated," he predicted, pushing the grumpy peacocks to their feet.

Since the goats were in a sound sleep, buckets of cold water were needed to rouse them. They turned their wet snouts pleadingly toward the loyal followers, but what could anyone do? The swami was in a crazed and maddened state. He babbled on about holy currents and stewed soup. There was nothing to do but allow oneself to be herded rudely into the elevator, and to pass with as much grace as possible through the lobby, under the incredulous eyes of the night desk clerk. What must he have thought with all of them in their underwear and trying to comb their beards with their fingers?

As it turned out, the night desk clerk was an angel in disguise. He rose magnificently to the occasion. In a short time he had corralled a fleet of taxis to carry the swami's troops to the airport. In addition, he wrote down long lists of things the loyal followers told him they had forgotten in their room: goat brushes, toothbrushes, lucky stones, prayer wheels, travel clocks, cotton socks and so on.

"We're sorry, but it's not our fault," the followers said to the night desk clerk. "Our master gave us only sixty seconds to pack. We didn't even have time to get dressed properly."

"Pas de tout. Pas de tout." The night desk clerk waved their apologies aside. He said he would mail everything to the States. Then he made himself useful hunting for lost shoes, smoothing the peacock's ruffled feathers and doing a hundred other things to ease the tension of departure. Never had there been such a night desk clerk.

"He is only what to expect from the Ritz," the swami said smugly.

Everyone else agreed that the man was something special. When the swami charged the night clerk's tip on his American Express card, instead of paying him up front with hard cash, the followers hissed among themselves. What a small-minded and miserly thing to do after the night desk clerk's great kindness! The loyal followers were terribly embarrassed. They gathered in a group apart from the swami and took up a collection. It didn't amount to much, but the night desk clerk appeared genuinely pleased when they poured the change into his cupped hands.

And then they were off, riding through the night streets of Paris, which were cold, empty, and grimly lit. These streets looked the very opposite of the gay avenues down which the group had recently walked. The swami sank low into his seat, as does a man who sees his own folly.

The airport, when they reached it, appeared just as drab and unappetizing. Only a few hours ago it had seemed to blaze with lights, with unusual gifts and romantic activity. Now, all the restaurants and shops were closed, except for a seedy 24-hour duty-free boutique. The swami slunk past without looking.

With their stand-by tickets in hand, the loyal followers could not resist swarming inside the boutique to examine its wares: a boar-bristle shaving brush, a battery-powered, push-button dog, magazines with unsuitable women posed on the covers.

"Come along," the swami said. "You don't want anything in there." But, in the end, he found himself buying an expensive bottle of French perfume with a vague idea of laying it before the holy tree when he finally arrived. Not that a tree of such power would be swayed for a moment by such a trivial gift. Still, it is always pleasing to receive a present, and many a hard heart has been softened by such means, the swami thought.

By now the followers had read all the magazines and run down the dog's batteries. They were ready to leave the boutique. How exasperating to find the swami in the midst of buying more presents! For no apparent reason, he had picked out a gigantic tube of lavender-scented bath oil. As the followers watched, he tried to decide which of two ridiculous-looking paperweights to buy.

One was made of see-through plastic and showed the Eiffel Tower in a snowstorm when shaken. The other was made of metal and molded into the shape of an elephant foot. Or was it a tree stump? The swami peered at the paperweight closely while the loyal followers looked at their watches and then at each other in a long-suffering way.

"Come along, Holy Master. You really don't want those paperweights, do you?" one follower dared to suggest.

"If we are going to fly stand-by, it would be best if we stood by the gate, don't you think?" another inquired.

It was then, under the pressure of sixty impatient eyes, that the swami inadvertently dropped the elephant foot on his toe.

"Yee-oww!"

The toe was crushed. The swami could hardly walk.

"We will carry you!" cried the followers, eagerly. "We would be honored to carry you to the gate."

Without waiting for the swami's consent, they picked him up and took him off on their shoulders.

What an excellent way to travel! Not for the swami, who was rather uncomfortable, but for the followers. Now they could go wherever they wanted, stop whenever they wished, speed up, slow down as their own needs dictated.

They were at the gate in a matter of minutes and before long had reserved themselves first class seats on the next flight to America. Without the swami, it was all so easy.

The followers shook each other's hands in triumph. They looked up at the swami on their shoulders. He had fallen asleep. The poor fellow was all tired out. His head had dropped back against one of the followers' strong necks, and his turban was coming unwrapped.

The loyal followers tucked it back in. They smoothed his hot forehead with their hands. The swami looked so dear when he was asleep. The loyal followers decided to send out for pizza and cold drinks while they waited to board the plane.

"Do you think there is anything to this holy oak tree business?" one follower whispered to the group while the swami snored softly overhead.

"Probably not," a second answered. "The swami's imagination is like a team of wild horses, always running away with him."

"Still, there's no harm in going to look at the tree, is there?" a third follower asked.

No harm at all, they all agreed. They ate their pizza, prepared the goats and peacocks for baggage class, and finally climbed aboard the plane. As the seven-hour journey across the Atlantic Ocean began, the followers fell asleep in their seats and dreamed about their cozy cave near Bombay. Their dreams were so real that they thought they were home, and that the fantastic trip to America was a dream instead.

LONG AFTER midnight, in the dark hours before the dawn of his eightieth birthday, the farmer rose up in his bed with the shocking thought that he had forgotten to write his will.

This was a mistake. The farmer had written a will just last year. It lay in the files of a lawyer in town, signed, dated, official in every respect. The lawyer had been instructed to bring it out upon the farmer's death, to read it to his family and to see that the terms were followed.

But the farmer recalled nothing about this document. He might recall digging for pirate treasure seventy years ago, but he could not remember giving instructions to his lawyer much more recently. All of a sudden he sat straight up in his bed and his heart gave a wallop. He thought: "I have forgotten to write my will!"

It wasn't easy for the farmer to get up at such an hour. Where was the light switch? Where were his slippers and bathrobe? His knees turned stiff and unmanageable in the cold room. Where was the blasted heater? He tripped over it and almost fell down on his way to the bathroom.

"Don't break your neck, old fellow," he warned himself.

Lately, he had gotten into the habit of talking to himself, of standing apart from his old man-ness and giving it advice, or helping it through difficult moments. After all,

he, the farmer, was not an old man. He was the same as he

had always been: strong, hard-working, a good storyteller. His old man-ness was like another person who had come to live with him since his wife's death, a person who must be looked after and given special treatment.

"Put up those old legs of yours and take a rest," the farmer would tell the old man. "No need for you to go worrying yourself. Things'll come out all right. They always do. You make yourself a nice cup of chocolate and sit down."

This matter was more worrisome, though. Forgetting to write a will is a serious business. A family has got to be told what to do when a person dies, otherwise it might do the wrong thing. It might get into a fight. Land might get sold for a bad price. An important tree might get chopped down.

"Chopped down! Good heavens," muttered the farmer. "Why have I never thought of that before?" He sat hurriedly at his desk and took out paper and pen.

To Whom It May Concern, he wrote with a wobble at the top of the page. It didn't sound quite right. The electric heater was purring like a contented cat beneath the desk, giving off thick waves of heat. Ah! It felt so good. What was life really but a matter of having enough heat on a cold night? The farmer sighed and crossed out what he had written.

To My Dear Family, he wrote warmly.

A storm had been raging outside but now seemed to be

passing. The rain came lightly against the bedroom windows. The farmer felt so cozy in his room. It was hard to imagine that he wouldn't always be here. But he wouldn't. He had to face facts. He was getting on. Tomorrow was his eightieth birthday. He was expecting a surprise party from his grandchildren to celebrate.

Or was he?

"The trouble is, I can't be sure," said the farmer, looking at the matter squarely for the first time. "They live so far away. Travel is so difficult. Telephone lines can break. Letters are lost in the mail."

He cocked his head and listened for the dry winter rustle of the oak down the hill. He imagined it standing out in the dark like a sentry, guarding the countryside, weathering the storm, waiting for morning. That was a comforting thought, all right. The tree had stood by on the day he was born and it would go on when he left off, weathering, waiting, "Guarding my memory," murmured the farmer.

"And my memories," he added, casting his mind back across the scenes from his life that he had recalled and relived during the past weeks.

"And guarding the old stories," he went on, thinking how they were the oak's real treasure, uncovered all these many years and shining in the sun.

"But who will guard the oak?" asked the farmer, picking up his pen again. Suddenly he knew the answer and, crumpling up the paper he had written on, he took out another piece.

To My Dear Family and To the Fine People of Dimpole, he wrote.

Then, he proceeded to set forth the terms of his will, which were practically the same as the terms that lay in the lawyer's file in town except for one thing.

After the farmer had left his farmhouse to his first son, his land to his only daughter, his furniture and china to his second son and a small chunk of money to each of his grandchildren, he left his great tree and its field to the people of Dimpole.

In hopes that all of you who have grown up with the tree will see fit to care for and protect it, as I have cared for it and loved it all my life, he wrote. (He wondered if the town would erect a monument to his family. Or would a memorial plaque be better? As long as they didn't try to screw it into the side of the tree!)

In hopes that your children and your children's children will play beneath the tree and listen to the telling of its old stories, the farmer wrote, with the heater blazing away. (He wondered if he should order his ashes buried between the oak's roots. It was pleasant to think of how the children's feet would patter overhead. On the other hand, what with all the recent digging for pirate's treasure, perhaps he would feel safer in a regular graveyard.)

In hopes that . . .

But here the farmer slumped in his chair. He had been just about to give out his rule—thinking fondly of Dexter—that anything anybody found lying on the ground or in the ground near the Dimpole Oak, well, it was the finder's property. The farmer fell back in his chair, and a night deeper than the night outside swept around him.

As the last of the storm passed over the farmer's house and headed for the sea, a dark silence fell upon Dimpole. The houses of the town huddled soundlessly against the valley floor and inside the houses the people slept without moving in their beds. Dogs lay still on door mats. Canaries hung motionless in cages. Cats crouched unseen on window sills. (But Miss Hand's black Loopy had run off during the evening walk and not come back. Most likely he was hunting mole.)

Everything lay hidden under cover of darkness and sleep, and the Dimpole Oak was at the center, as silent and invisible as if it had never been there. Only in dreams did it rise up and show itself. Then it faded or changed into something else and the long, silent hours rolled on.

Would Saturday morning, October 25th never come?

It came—a prickle of light along the western horizon. Then the colors: pink, rose, lavender, lilac. Then a surge of brightness and finally the sun itself, nosing up over the hills, moving faster than expected and catching Dimpolers in various stages of waking up:

Mrs. Trawley, heaving herself mountainously out of bed and into a hot bath: "Ah-h-h. It's Great Dimpole Oak Day at last! 'Ladies and Gentlemen, I do not intend to bore you today with flowery language or metaphors on the nature of things . . .' "

Mr. Glover, the lovebird crooning over his coffee:

"George Washington rode underneath that tree and nodded to it. I know it as well as I know that Shirley Hand kissed me there last night. Oh, what a beautiful morning!"

And Shirley Hand in her tiny apartment, her heavy-lashed eyes just opening on the day: "What a romantic place! What a romantic man! But Loopy has run off. I think he was jealous of Harvey. Will we ever find him? Will we?"

And Dexter and Howlie—Howlie peering through binoculars at the oak across rosy-colored fields:

"Can you see Bulldog?"

"Nope."

"Are you sure he's coming?"

"Never said he wasn't."

"Have you got your blood bag on?"

"Yup."

"Have you got your knife?"

"Yup."

"Are you scared?"

"Nope."

"Are you still mad at me, Howlie?"

"I'm deciding."

5

MR. GLOVER WAS RIGHT. The morning that rose over Dimpole that day was clear, blue and perfectly beautiful. Anyone would have agreed, even someone who wasn't in love with a gorgeous, talented, lavender-scented teacher named Shirley Hand.

The storm had vanished and there was no sign of how it had raged across the valley. Or rather, there seemed to be no sign while the light remained weak. But when the sun's full rays struck the land, one difference could be plainly seen. The Dimpole Oak was stripped of leaves. The last of its crop had blown off in the wind. The tree's great arms mounted bare and black against the brightening sky.

"Holy cow. Look at the oak," said Dexter Drake on his stomach in the field below the tree. He handed the binoculars to Howlie.

"Not a leaf left on it," Howlie said. "It looks sort of sad or embarrassed standing out there with nothing on, don't you think?"

Dexter snorted. "There's nothing sad about that oak. If you ask me, it's got an evil streak in it. You should have seen it last night waving its arms around and creaking. I had the strangest feeling it was after me for some reason. Even now, it looks kind of horrible, like a black hand stuck down in the ground."

"You're weird," said Howlie.

"You know what? I bet there *are* diamonds buried under the tree," Dexter went on. "There's probably a lot of other stuff, too. But nobody will ever find anything because the tree wants to have it for itself. It's sitting up there on top of everything keeping watch, and anyone who comes too close gets the treatment."

"What treatment?" asked Howlie.

"The scare treatment. You think I'm kidding but you weren't there last night. The whole tree came alive."

"You're beginning to sound exactly like the farmer," said Howlie. "Next you'll be telling me there's human blood in its branches."

"There is," said Dexter. "And human sweat and human
 tears. The farmer is one hundred per cent on target. This

oak is on the look-out for human parts. It's standing there waiting to get its hands on them."

"Well, maybe it got all of Bulldog Calhoun at once," said Howlie, bringing the conversation back to business. "I don't see any sign of him."

Dexter took up the binoculars and surveyed the area.

"Something else is funny," he said. "There have been lights on upstairs in the farmer's house since before we got here."

"He probably gets up early," Howlie said.

Dexter shrugged. "It seems strange for him to have all the lights on so early in the morning. And why hasn't he turned them off by now? The sun is pouring through his windows."

Dexter peered through the glasses again.

"I can't see any movement in there," he said.

"Maybe he's watching TV."

"Howlie?" said Dexter. He put his hand on his friend's shoulder. "I know you're going to kill me for this." He raised a finger to his forehead and shot himself. "I don't want you to think I'm running out on our fight-to-the-death plan."

"Oh no, not again," Howlie said.

"It's probably nothing, but the farmer didn't look too well yesterday when I saw him. I think I should go check him out. See, he's got nobody. Not even a dog. It hit me when I went to see him about the treasure. He pretends he doesn't care but he's all by himself. If anything happened . . ."

"Not now," said Howlie. "Please don't go now."

"I'll be right back, honest. When Bulldog shows up, just keep him talking until I come."

"You want me to keep Bulldog talking?" Howlie said. "When was the last time anyone ever talked to Bulldog?"

"I'll be right back," yelled Dexter as he ran toward the farmhouse. "I've just got to do this one thing."

"Dexter Drake you are an oversized rat of the hairiest kind!" Howlie howled after him. "If I'm dead when you get back, I'm holding you personally responsible."

DEXTER hadn't been gone more than five minutes when Howlie began to hear noises coming from the direction of the main road: car doors slamming and a burble of voices. He rose to his knees and swung the glasses around to have a look.

Bulldog was nowhere in sight, but down on the road people seemed to be arriving. Howlie focused the binoculars and leaned forward. They were parking their cars on the edge of the pavement and getting out. Some were laughing and shaking hands. Others stood apart and gazed up the hill toward the big oak tree. Howlie ducked. A great fear swept over him. He knew who they were looking for.

Every minute, more people arrived. Whole families were unloading from station wagons. Tiny children were being buckled into strollers. Larger children galloped between the cars. Someone pulled a whole bunch of helium-filled balloons from the back of a van. When the children saw this, they galloped over with hoots and squeals to surround the balloonman. Then:

"Boom! Boom! Boom!" Howlie shot to his feet and panned the roadside. Far down the ever lengthening line of parked vehicles he saw two people carrying a big bass drum. While he watched, one person helped the other person put on a chest harness and attach the drum to it.

"Boom! Boom! Boom!" The person wearing the drum hit it with a padded drumstick.

"That's the bass drum from the high school," Howlie said out loud in horror. He turned around and began to run toward the farmer's, shouting.

"Dexter! Help! They've come to watch us fight!
People are here. Wait up!
They've even got
a drum!"

When Mrs. Trawley heard the first boom of the bass drum she'd ordered up from the high school, her plump cheeks trembled and she had to blink her eyes quickly.

"Hear that?" she asked the group of volunteer workers standing around her. "It's the drum and it's here right on time. I said to be here at 8:30 sharp and it is."

"On time?" murmured the group.

"That may sound funny to say," Mrs. Trawley went on, "but I can tell you from experience that things don't always go so smoothly in organizing. There you are juggling a hundred little details and then something gets out of line and oh, what a mess. What a mess!"

Mrs. Trawley wiped at her eyes as if some specks of dust had blown in them.

"Do you know that there have been times during the last week when I didn't see, no, I honestly didn't see how Great Dimpole Oak Day would ever get off the ground," she confessed with a quiver in her voice.

The volunteers stepped back and looked at her in amazement. Could this be true? No, it couldn't. How could Mrs. Trawley, the one-woman powerhouse, their fearless leader, have doubts? She was being modest. She was overtired. The volunteers glanced at her nervously and hoped she wasn't losing her mind.

"I'll tell you something else, too," Mrs. Trawley said, while the volunteers took another step up the road away from her. "I would never have come through except for the thought of the terrible farmer and his neglect of our dear tree. Always I kept this before me: the Dimpole Oak is in grave danger. I must save it. I must!"

Her words were punctuated by another series of booms from the bass drum, giving them an extra ring of importance. The volunteers heaved a sigh of relief. They moved back to surround her. Here was the Mrs. Trawley they knew. She was in command. Now the march could begin.

And in a matter of minutes it did begin. It had to begin, for by now some three hundred Dimpolers, men, women and children, had arrived and the roadside could no longer contain them all. They spilled over onto the road where they would have been run down or caused a traffic jam if the Dimpole Police had not been there to control them. Really, one had to hand it to Mrs. Trawley, she had thought of everything.

"Boom! Boom! Boom-bumpa-boom!"

The bass drum set the marching beat. Hundreds of feet fell into step. The most direct route to the oak seemed to be up the farmer's driveway. Was he watching? Fortunately, his farmhouse was located up the slope from the tree so no one would have to march under his very windows.

"Boom! Boom! Boom-bumpa-boom!"

Some of the marchers' posters were quite ingenious. One read: "Free the Tree!" and showed a picture of the

Dimpole Oak with wings on, escaping from a giant bird cage.

In another, a figure closely resembling the farmer was chopping down the oak with an ax while a child stood by weeping. Underneath, the caption said: "Once upon a time there was a nasty old man who lived all by himself on the edge of a town."

Another sign proclaimed:

"We'll guard our oak
Until we croak."

"Boom! Boom!" The marchers tramped up the driveway, two and three abreast. No sooner had the first in line reached the tree than Mrs. Trawley's voice could be heard rising above all, ordering the speaker's podium put down there, the popcorn booth set up here, and so on. Not one detail had been forgotten. Not one bottle of soda was missing. Every volunteer had performed his or her job (although many had needed extra prodding). But—where was Miss Hand, who was in charge of the Special Entertainment? Mrs. Trawley looked around and could not see her.

"I hope Miss Hand has not overslept," she said to a passing volunteer. She did not have time to worry because suddenly a host of other problems bore down upon her:

The ground under the oak tree was unaccountably riddled with holes and strewn with dirt piles, which made walking there all but impossible.

The leg of an important card table fell into one of the holes and snapped off.

A box full of little American flags to be passed out after the speeches was missing.

The screws for the Abraham Lincoln plaque were still in Mr. Glover's possession and he was missing, too.

"Oh, dear! Oh, dear!" Mrs. Trawley massaged her temples and gazed up, as if seeking help, into the branches of the great tree. There her eye caught sight of a large, black, furry animal watching her from one of the lower limbs.

Oh, help! Even as Mrs. Trawley opened her mouth to scream, the black panther rose on its haunches and prepared to spring.

"Help! Help! Oh, help!"

Mrs. Trawley fainted. She collapsed neatly onto the top of one of Dexter's dirt piles. How convenient, after all, to have it there.

"HARVEY, MY LOVE. What is that strange procession coming toward us?" said Miss Hand, as she looked across the fields that swept up to the Dimpole Oak.

"Where?" asked Mr. Glover. He was bent over locking the car door. They were only just arriving at the rally, half an hour late, due to a number of long, passionate unforeseen circumstances in the post office that morning. Also, they had forgotten the cat cage, which would be needed if Loopy should reappear at the tree, and they had gone back to Miss Hand's apartment to get it. This had led to further circumstances, admittedly more foreseeable by this time.

"Over there." Miss Hand shaded her eyes from the sun. "It looks like a herd of something, and some peacocks, and people wearing turbans."

"What?" exclaimed Mr. Glover, turning around.

"And they are carrying something. No. Someone," Miss Hand went on. "Let's go see who it is." She started walking across the stubbly field.

"Yoo hoo! Over here," Miss Hand called. The herd was making a bee-line for the rally and was about to pass in front of her. It came to a halt and, swaying like a parade-day float forced to pause in mid-course, waited for Miss Hand and Mr. Glover to come up.

"Are you lost, by any chance?" Miss Hand called politely as she approached.

"Can we help you with directions or an address?" asked Mr. Glover with more menace in his voice.

Immediately it became clear that none of the group spoke English, unless perhaps the white-bearded fellow being carried aloft. But he was sound asleep and would not wake up, even when the others shook him. Miss Hand did not know what to do next. She wondered if she should resort to sign language.

"Have you come very far?" she asked, gesturing shyly at the horizon.

There was every indication of a difficult journey. The travelers were all bone-thin, and their toes, which stuck out from the ends of their worn sandals, were caked with mud. Further, they were not dressed warmly, considering the day's coolness, and their clothing, fascinating though it was, did not look very clean.

"I can't imagine who they are or why they have turned up here, of all places," Mr. Glover told Miss Hand in a low voice. He eyed one of the goats with distaste. "Someone will have to be notified. They can't be allowed to wander aimlessly around the countryside like a traveling circus."

"Traveling circus!" exclaimed Miss Hand.

"Or a gypsy caravan."

"Oh!" Miss Hand looked at the group with new interest.

"Actually," said Mr. Glover, drawing her aside protectively, "they look like a bunch of snake charmers to me. I'd be careful of my purse if I were you."

"Snake charmers!" cried Miss Hand. "Oh, Harvey, what a brilliant idea. It's just what I've been praying for. They are the perfect Special Entertainment. Look at them. I am saved!"

Before Mr. Glover could advise her against it, Miss Hand began to tell the herd in vigorous sign language that it was invited to a party. Everyone was invited to the rally taking place that very minute under the big oak tree. And the drinks and popcorn were on the house. (She made gobbling and gurgling noises and rubbed her stomach.) And the goats could graze in any field they wished. (She lowered her head and pretended to chew grass.) And the peacocks were free to peck and scratch or do whatever peacocks do. (Miss Hand had never been sure what they did.)

"Follow me!" she cried at last, setting off with her arm hooked through Mr. Glover's.

The vast float of animals and people started to move across the field again. It went slowly to begin with, hobbling and wobbling in places. But gradually it gathered speed, and with speed its size appeared to increase and its expression grew fierce, and the earth shook as it thundered along. Meanwhile, at the tree, the townsfolk heard a rumbling noise and turned around just in time to see a furious throng of wild-eyed, cleft-footed, feathery barbarians sweeping down upon them.

Luckily, the impression lasted only a few seconds. Then, Miss Hand could be seen detaching herself from the throng, smiling in triumph and introducing the newcomers. Mrs. Trawley, who had been on the verge of a second faint, came forward to congratulate her, and to start organizing before anything could go wrong.

"You may set up your tables and equipment over there," she told the groggy swami, whom she had mistaken for a fortune teller because of his turban.

The swami had been awakened by the wild dash across the fields and was just opening his eyes to look about.

"Over there," Mrs. Trawley insisted, pointing to a patch of field on the farmhouse side of the oak. "And let me remind you," she added, glancing at him shrewdly, "that fifty per cent of whatever profit you make from your show must be donated to the Great Dimpole Oak Preservation Fund. I don't want to put you out of business, but money is a consideration here."

The swami rubbed his eyes and stared at Mrs. Trawley as if she were herself a feathery barbarian. Then, his gaze shifted and he focused for the first time on the enormous trunk of the tree in back of her.

"So," murmured the swami in a foreign tongue that made Mrs. Trawley's eyebrows furrow with suspicion. "We have arrived."

"Holy Master, this place isn't bad at all," the loyal followers chorused. "They have offered us free food and camp land. We're starving, so if you don't mind we'll just dump you off here and . . ."

The swami raised his hand. "One moment, please," he asked them. "I must first make my presence known to the tree."

Then, up and up his eyes went, following the lines of the great limbs, the curves of the slim branches, the fingers of the littlest twigs, up, up and endlessly up to the blue sky overhead and the horizon far away. (He thought of Bombay.) And his eyes came down with tears in them and swept across the valley, across the fields, across the farmer's house, his barn, back to the oak's trunk again. Here, the swami noticed in passing that he and his loyal followers were not the only ones who had come to worship. Who were all these people? And dressed so oddly. And staring at him with saucer-shaped eyes. He signaled his followers to put him down.

The moment his feet hit the ground, the swami's eyes flashed like an ancient wizard's and he felt his old power rise up in him and take command. Oh, it felt so good! Apparently he was forgiven everything, even that outrageous behavior in Paris. The swami lifted his arms in thanks toward the great tree. While his followers munched popcorn and every other man, woman and child at the rally looked on with amazement, the swami bent in two and kissed the ground.

 The holy red current was everywhere. He saw it flickering in the earth under the tree, surging through the roots, crackling along the branches. Good heavens, the place was thick with it. It was dangerous to stand in one place for too long, he discovered, lest the soles of his feet become scorched.

The swami mopped his brow and began to chant. It seemed the only way to control the current's force. He raised his arms like a powerful bird about to take flight. He walked underneath the tree. Dexter's holes did not bother him in the least. He went across them as if they had never been dug, as if they were solid ground.

While the whole crowd watched, the swami performed a daring series of athletic movements designed to focus his spirit and to exercise his double joints. (He was showing off just a little, for the benefit of the oak.)

He took a small box wrapped in gold paper from beneath his garments and laid it down between some roots.

The swami walked in a circle all the way around
the oak, chanting as he went, filled up with
new holiness, his high-pitched voice
streaming out single-
mindedly across
the valley.

MEANWHILE, at a second floor window in the farmhouse above the rally, curtains parted and the glassy eyes of a pair of binoculars looked out.

They zeroed in on the action under the tree, focusing first on the singing swami, next on the hypnotized audience, on the goats grazing, the peacocks fanning, on Mrs. Trawley beside the podium drumming her fingers, on Mr. Glover and Miss Hand sneaking off together behind the oak, on some children giggling in a hole and, finally, on a large black cat carrying a large dead mole into the bushes.

"So, this is Great Dimpole Oak Day. Unbelievable. Everything known to man is going on down there," Dexter Drake said to his friend Howlie Howlenburg. "And look. There's the cat I saw last night. That makes me feel better. I thought I was seeing things."

"Talk about seeing things, those goats look amazingly like the wild Tibetan mountain goats I wrote my report on last week," said Howlie. "But how could that be? Dimpole is thousands of miles out of their range."

"Stranger things have happened," answered Dexter. "For instance, at this very moment Miss Matterhorn is riding the root."

"Where? Let me have those binoculars."

"She's not very good, but not completely terrible either," said Dexter. "It looks as if she may have had some practice."

"Practice!" Howlie put his hand over his mouth and wheezed.

"If you're talking about Gertrude Matterhorn, she used to be one of the best root riders in town," said a voice behind the boys.

They turned around. "Are you kidding?" said Dexter.

"No," replied the farmer from his bed. "No one could ride the root the way Trudy could. I used to stand out and watch her, same as I watched all you kids to make sure you didn't crack your heads open. She was bigger than all the boys, of course, and she had a pair of legs that would shoot her straight up in the air like a grasshopper."

"She's still got them," said Dexter, peering through the glasses. "Who would have ever guessed?"

"I'd better get up and take a look after all these years," said the farmer, raising himself from the pillow. But the boys were beside him in a flash.

"Don't get up!" ordered Dexter. "You're supposed to stay quiet till the doctor gets here. He told us on the phone."

"We almost lost you once and we're not going through that again," said Howlie, laying a hand on the farmer's shoulder. "Do you know we thought you were dead when we first came in this room? You were all crumpled up in your chair with your arms dangling down. It really scared us."

"Dead!" The farmer gave a snort. "I got an overdose of

heat is all. That blasted heater is supposed to turn off when it gets too hot in here. It never does a thing it's supposed to do. Anyway," the farmer went on, raising himself once again, "I'm getting up whether you like it or not. I've got a right to see my own party, haven't I? And besides, I've got an announcement to make."

"I'm not sure it's your party, exactly," murmured Dexter, while he and Howlie glanced at each other over his white head like a pair of worried surgeons.

"Of course it is!" the farmer said. He shuffled across to the window in his pajamas. "And look at all the people!" he cried. "The whole town has turned out for my eightieth birthday. You can't beat that. Look at the balloons. Look at the streamers. Is that a peacock scratching in my garden?"

At this point, the farmer opened the window and began to call to people outside and wave to passing children. Immediately, Dexter and Howlie reached to draw him back inside before he discovered the true nature of the rally. But the old man pushed them away and refused to be quiet.

"What'll we do?" Dexter whispered to Howlie. "This rally looks like a lot of people having fun, but underneath it's pretty nasty. Have you seen the signs and posters?"

"There's nothing we can do," Howlie answered, "except hope the farmer goes on thinking it's his birthday. You know how it is when you get an idea in your head. Maybe he'll never guess."

"It is amazing what you can talk yourself into," Dexter whispered back. "There I was yesterday believing that a bunch of diamonds was talking to me!"

"That's right," said Howlie. "And what about me this morning? When I saw everyone getting out of their cars on the road I was sure they were coming to watch us fight to the death. The real death, while the drum rolled. Isn't it strange how you can see things in different ways?"

Dexter nodded, then said: "I've been watching that big woman, Mrs. Trawley, hanging around the platform they put up down there. She's getting ready to give a speech, and when she does, it'll blow the whole birthday party idea to pieces. If we could just get the farmer back in bed before it starts . . ."

"Or somehow interrupt the speech . . ." Howlie put in.

"Great idea! Let's wait and see what happens."

The boys went back to the window to stand protectively behind their invalid, who was not acting very sick and was certainly not bothering to wait for the doctor. He had struck up a conversation with the singing swami, who had wandered up toward the house looking for a higher point from which to view the great tree.

". . . It all came up the trunk, it did, from things that happened right there under the tree," the farmer was telling the holy man.

"Really?" the swami replied. He sat down and rubbed his foot soles.

RJ
SG

JTL

"See those branches up there waving in the wind? There's blood in them, yessir, family and blood."

"Blood!" the swami exclaimed. "That's a new idea, all right. You wouldn't happen to have a pail of water around somewhere, would you? I'm scorching to death out here."

"I'll be right down," said the farmer. "I've got an announcement to make anyhow, and I'd be glad to fill up a pail. Where are you from, if I may ask? I'm so pleased you could make it to my birthday party."

At this moment, the drum from the high school sounded: "Boom! Boom! Boom!" The crowds, which up until then had been milling vaguely around the swami's loyal followers, began to assemble with more certainty in front of Mrs. Trawley's podium. Since there were no chairs, people sat on the grass, or on a root, or they leaned against the oak tree munching popcorn.

"Boom! Boom!" The goats were terrified of the drum. They bolted whenever it was beaten and ran off in a thunder of hoofs. And when the goats stampeded the peacocks became upset and screamed, which in turn made the smaller children weep with fright. Altogether, quite a lot of noise came up from the rally, so that when Mrs. Trawley finally climbed the podium and asked for silence, several minutes passed before she got it.

"Ladies and Gentlemen!" cried the tireless woman.

She was pleased to see that she had finally attracted

 people's attention away from Miss Hand's high-powered

zombie. Really, the man was a perfect menace. Between his ear-splitting wails and his gymnastics, he had almost obscured the whole point of the rally. Furthermore, his workers had proved to be an undisciplined band of free-loaders. Even now, out of the corner of her eye, she noticed that they were occupying the popcorn stand, eating five bags for every one they sold.

Mrs. Trawley cleared her throat: ahem!

"Ladies and Gentlemen. I do not intend to bore you today with flowery language or extended metaphors on the nature of things. Let me go right to the point and say that the reason I have organized this excellent rally . . ."

What was that scuffle going on at the back of the audience? Mrs. Trawley glanced up but did not let it distract her.

". . . the reason you are all here listening to me attentively . . ."

From the audience came more stirrings, and muffled voices: "Excuse us. Let us through. Pardon me. We need to get up front." Mrs. Trawley charged ahead at full volume.

". . . the reason I am standing up here singlehandedly giving this great speech is that . . ."

"Coming through," said Dexter's voice.

"Please clear the way for my good friend, the farmer. We older men need breathing space," said the swami's voice in its thick Indian accent.

Mrs. Trawley cleared her throat again.

". . . is that . . . is that . . ."

She got no further in her speech because suddenly people were jumping up and talking at once, and calling and reaching to shake the farmer's hand as he passed between them in his bathrobe and slippers. Everyone was pleased to see the old man. Now that he was here among them in the flesh, they forgot his crimes against the oak (whatever they were; it had never been entirely clear). They remembered the stories he had told them as children. They remembered his kind, gruff manner. But he was looking so gaunt and wrinkly. Not at all well, no, and spending time in bed. What a shame!

The farmer arrived on the podium with a thud, propelled by eager hands.

"Oh!" said Mrs. Trawley. "It's you."

The farmer nodded, and though she tried to back away he grasped her hand and shook it warmly.

"Thank you for everything," he told her, while she stared at him as if he had lost his mind. "I understand you are the one who has arranged this wonderful party for me. I appreciate it deeply. As it happens, I have an announcement to make to you and everyone here. Do you mind if I step up before the microphone? My voice is not strong and my kind young bodyguards," he glanced over at Howlie and Dexter, who blushed to be pointed out in public, "are threatening to drag me off to a hospital at any moment."

The farmer spread his arms wide. The crowd fell instantly silent.

"My dear friends, I have had the most wonderful idea!" he began, and proceeded to announce his plan to leave the Dimpole Oak to the fine people of Dimpole, in hopes that they would care for and protect it, as he had done all his life.

"We will!" shouted several voices in the crowd.

In hopes that the children would play beneath the tree and keep its stories and memories alive with telling and listening, the farmer said.

"They will!" roared the crowd. Some of the softer-hearted members of the audience, recalling their childhood years, took handkerchiefs from their pockets and blotted their eyes.

The farmer waited for the noise and the blotting to die down, then he said, quietly, looking about at the children:

"There is one condition. It's the rule around here and always has been that anything anybody finds lying on the ground or in the ground near the tree, well, it's the finder's property. And the finder can do with it as he wishes. And no one has the right to tell him otherwise. And this," the farmer said, even more quietly, "includes pirate treasure."

"Pirate treasure!" screamed all the children, jumping to their feet. "Is that story true?"

They raced for the foot of the tree and began to examine Dexter's holes and to pry into other likely places, which forced the farmer to remind them sternly not to dig up the great oak's roots.

Afterwards, he descended from the podium and was given a hero's welcome by the people of Dimpole. Certainly, he would go down in history as the kindest and most generous man in the town. Everyone wondered how they had ever thought of him in any other way.

And Dexter and Howlie were given heroes' welcomes by association, because the farmer had pointed them out on the podium. But after they explained, modestly, that they had rescued the farmer from a crazed electric heater, and that they were at any moment going to call the hospital if the doctor didn't show up, then Dimpolers looked at them with even more respect.

"I hope Bulldog is here somewhere watching us," Howlie said to Dexter as they walked through the throngs receiving congratulations.

But Dexter didn't hear him. He had just taken a knife out of his pocket and stabbed himself in the stomach. While the children under the tree watched in horror, he reeled with a cry, grabbed desperately for Howlie's shoulder, missed, crumpled up, fell to the ground and lay writhing in a pool of fire-engine red blood.

Howlie folded his arms across his chest and rolled his eyes away from this tragic scene in embarrassment.

Up on the podium, Mrs. Trawley tucked the Abraham Lincoln memorial plaque under one arm and shook hands with the other.

"Thank you. Thank you. Yes, we have won our first victory," she told well-wishers. "But this is only the beginning. We have years more of organizing ahead of us. Years of hard work and herding—ahem!—I mean hosting fund-raiser dinners. The Dimpole Oak has a blazing future before it. And just wait until I mount this handsome plaque. I am sorry it can't be done today. You see, the screws are missing."

In a romantic scene behind the oak, another kind of memorial was being created, however. Bent over, with their heads close together, Miss Hand and Mr. Glover were putting the finishing touches on a large heart they had carved into the tree's trunk with Miss Hand's monogrammed jackknife. ("What else do you carry in your purse?" Mr. Glover had asked her in all seriousness.) Inside the heart, they had carved their initials: HG & SH.

"Now this day will go down in history, and so will we," sighed Miss Hand, while Mr. Glover pocketed the jackknife. "And, if we can just find my dear cat Loopy, all will be right with the world."

"That cat is a nuisance," said Mr. Glover through his teeth. "We have spent the entire day looking for it. I'm beginning to believe that you think more of it than you do of me." He walked off in the direction of his car.

"Harvey, what an idiotic thing to say!" exclaimed Miss Hand, running after him. They disappeared down the farmer's driveway, arguing with each other.

By now, the sun had begun to set and the Great Dimpole

Oak was casting long, black shadows across the field. People hastened to gather their belongings, to pack up the popcorn stand and dismantle the bass drum. They dragged their children out of the treasure holes (as they were ever after called) and went away down the hill, tired and hungry.

"Goodbye!" cried the children to the swami's loyal followers, who were the only ones left under the tree. They looked a little like children themselves, with lost expressions on their faces.

"Holy Master!" the followers called into the gathering gloom. "Where are you? Everyone else has gone and they have taken our popcorn stand and it's getting dark. You wouldn't leave us out here with this monster of a tree, would you?"

Unfortunately, the swami was in the farmer's kitchen, where he had been invited, along with Howlie and Dexter, to cook dinner for the farmer and keep him company after the doctor's visit. They were telling stories.

The loyal followers stamped their feet angrily. They invoked the ghost of Napoleon. After a while, they went away to the campgrounds that Mrs. Trawley had given them and lit fires, over which they huddled and spoke of dumping the swami permanently.

So Great Dimpole Oak Day came to an end, with varying degrees of success. But the great oak itself went on
 standing in the field, as it did at the end of every day. It

took on the colors of the sunset, which were fiery, fall ones. When the sun had gone down, it absorbed the fading purples of the hills. Just then, a red moon crested the darkening horizon. Far away, a cat screamed. The wind around the oak seemed suddenly full of whispers.

Or was this only in someone's imagination?

Also by Janet Taylor Lisle

The Dancing Cats of Applesap

Sirens and Spies